Hockey Rules!

David Hadasz

PublishAmerica
Baltimore

ISBN: 1-4241-8924-1
PUBLISHED BY PUBLISHAMERICA, LLLP
www.publishamerica.com
Baltimore

Printed in the United States of America

Hockey Rules!

Chapter One: Birth of Area Hockey

Utica, New York. Once known as "Sin City" for the Italian life Mafia and crime in the streets. Located near three different prisons, ideal for outside criminals and family members to visit, and staying in hotels in the city. Now known as the "Doughnut City," not because we have good bakery shops or hungry police officers, but because of the good suburban areas that surround the city. You see, Utica is a nice city but a lot of the old vacant buildings make the city look like one big hole in the middle. The suburbs are really pleasant areas, mostly middle-class living and up, with shopping malls, centers, plazas, and a few attractions here and there.

Bleecker St. Vacant factories and boarded up windows of buildings, once a very hopping place with over 90,000 residents located in the center of NY State. Now populated with a quarter less with deserted buildings, shops and markets. Old photographic memories remain of the workers in the downtown area in the 50s and 60s. Busy intersections, eighteen-story hotels, many billboards located on roofs of the buildings, crowded streets, trolley heading down Genesee St. train station filled with patrons at the bar, mostly men with top hats, playing cards and having a drink or two while waiting.

Down Oriskany Blvd. Across from the Utica Police Department, stands the newly constructed Utica Arena, standing in the heart of the city. Two men work in front of the arena with tools stamping 1954 into one of the last cement blocks that was placed in front of the pillars of the front entrance.

Standing at the podium in front of the arena is the mayor, standing front wise of 100s of people, some with signs: "Welcome Hockey" and "Thank you Mayor Miller" shouting out in markers.

"This city has come a long way," Miller said. "We have grace, dignity, culture. What else can you ask for? How about a hockey team, I do declare to play for our own home town city!"

He raised his hands to the drop down logo above and behind him. "I bring you the Utica Snakes Hockey Club."

Cheers rolling like thunder as the fans express their feelings to this new era of entertainment never seen in person before. Men throwing hats in the air, and cars honking their horns in the parking lot nearby.

Being seen all of this on a color TV screen, as technology transposed this from black and white, Kyle watched all this on his 36 inch wide screen HD-LG-TV.

"How the fuck did these people spread the news so fast without cell phones and computers?" he questioned to himself.

Moments later the phone rings. Stuffing his face with Chex Mix, he leans over to pick up the goalie masked hockey phone.

A very sophisticated Englishman's voice can be heard: "Excuse me, sire, but your ride is out front and patiently awaiting your presence."

"Oh shit...I'll grab my wienie and be down with the jiff!" Kyle said frantically. He sprinted into the kitchen, grabbed a hot dog out of the freezer and stuck it into the microwave to nuke it. In the meantime, he threw on his brown and orange Utica Snakes hockey jersey, jumped over the couch (which was actually bleacher seats from an old hockey arena) and tripped over the junk on the floor. Yes, his apartment was quite a mess. He ran into the bedroom and grabbed a hockey stick wrapped in cloth on half of it, and darted back into the kitchen, the microwave beeping, he grabbed his so-called weenie, burning his fingertips, threw it onto the countertop. He quickly spread on the Jiffy peanut butter, squeezed the jelly on it, wrapped it into a bun, and ran for the door, throwing a piece of his hot dog to his dog "Probert."

Once out the door, he stopped dead in his tracks, looked at the chauffeur standing out of the sun roof of a rusty old 1985 Oldsmobile Delta with a Snakes cap on, and with an English accent again, he bowed tipping his hat. "At your service, sir."

Kyle grinned at his faked accent buddy Jared. "To the bloody game!"

"Fuckin' eh!" Jarred proclaimed, throwing his fist in the air. Kyle jumped threw the passenger window head first.

Cranking up the radio on the way to the game, Kyle unrolled the cloth from his hockey stick and stuck it out the sun roof of the car. The colors of orange and brown unveiled the Snakes logo and stripes. Kyle and Jared were beating to the beat of the heavy metal band Godsmack, being the lip sync artists that they felt they could be, as they cruised their way down the boulevard en route to the Snakes game.

Chapter Two: Snake Hockey

"Odds are in favor tonight that you guys will be getting into mischief," the ticket taker said to Jared and Kyle as they handed them their tickets.

Kyle looked at the burley ticket taker and patted him on the shoulder. "If that is the case, I hope this mischief is a cute redhead with fine ass curves," he said while grinning.

The boys walked through the lobby area with their heads up high, holding their brown and yellow Snakes hockey stick flag, a cup of beer each and their brown and yellow Snakes caps and jerseys. Jared was wearing #69 home jersey and Kyle fashioning off the #0. Jared had the hairstyle of the 70s style of today with brown hair and a five o'clock shadow. Kyle, on the other hand, had a mullet type style, but was shagged on the sides. Both stood at about five feet ten inches tall.

"Crush 'em tonight!" claimed a fan walking next to them as they both high five him. Another fan crossing their way from head-on puts his fists in the air and Kyle high fisted him back as a mean style of high five.

"We gotta win at least one game this month," joked the fan.

The lobby of the arena was somewhat vacant but the fans there all seemed to know Jared and Kyle. They were the guys that got the crowds on their feet, started chants, got the cheers and had the entertainment when it wasn't provided on the ice.

As Jared and Kyle approached their usual section, they

darted straight down to the glass where they sit in their front row seats. Their season ticket seats are right next to the visiting team's penalty box on the side of the rink. The players were all on the ice warming up before the game. You could see the big handmade sign that some fans made right above the section that read: "Welcome to the Snake Pit."

Jared made thumbs up jester to Tory Hatch through the glass. Hatch was the team's enforcer. The six-foot-three, two-hundred-and-thirty pound tough guy from Ontario of the great white north. Hatch nodded in reply to them. Kyle and Jared both yelled and high fived one another of their accomplishment. They had a great buddy to buddy relationship with the Snakes players, at least in their own minds. The players knew who they were, but what they were, was a different story from another world. But the players knew those boys were dedicated fans and helped contribute to their paychecks.

The arena sat only about 4,000 but was perfect size for this city. The seats did not go all the way around the rink as it had a classic "stage" end. The scoreboard above was old, but served its purpose. Some of the lights were out on it but was readable for the fans. The dasher boards were naked in most areas as only the local brewery and a couple dealerships and supermarkets supported them.

The lights went down as the national anthem began. As the Saginaw starting lineup was standing on the blue line, as normal for the song, Kyle and Jared were just about ten feet away from them. Standing against the glass as it only reached to their necks, they began heckling their visiting arch rivals. #9 was closest to them. Standing at the blue line, helmet off and holding in one hand, stick in the other, only the sound of the singer is heard.

"Psssst...pssst...pssssssst," the guys were whispering

sounds loudly. A couple of the fans behind them starting snickering as #9 could do anything but to look up to see who was trying to get his undivided attention and why.

"Psssst…#9, hey you look up here to your left." He slowly turned his head, looking out the corner of his eyes.

"Duh!" yelled Jared. The player shook his head, looked down, his glove in hand was in stroking motion back and forth at the front of his protective cup.

Kyle yelled, "Do you mean to tell me that you know what your wife did to me before we came here?" The Snake Pit fans in their section chuckled as the player got ticked off but couldn't do anything. This is what that section is all about. Breakin' balls, having a good time, and in hopes to throw the opposing players off their game to help their team win some games! That is what was in the minds of the Snake Pit, section 113, at the Utica Arena. According to the WUTC News, the Snake Pit is the loudest, rowdiest and most fun section to sit. It is fully sold out by season ticket holders who are there for every game.

"I'm Marc Jackson and welcome to another divisional match-up between the Saginaw Blast and your Utica Snakes," stated the Snakes radio announcer in the booth high up above the last row of seats in the side end of the arena. "The barn is almost half full in capacity, well…if you put the ushers, venders and players into the seats as well," he said sarcastically. "Tonight's game brought to you by Dax beer, the beer for your cheer!" advertised Jackson.

"The puck is ready to be dropped, like a raw piece of meat between two pit bulls…and we are off."

It didn't take long before the Snakes were already down by two goals. The fans, with the exception of the Snake Pit, were silent like a morgue. Between face-offs, the loud system was playing slow love songs. Something you haven't heard from in years and definitely didn't want to hear at a hockey game. Just as the horn blew for the end of the second period, one of the blast players took a vicious hit on the Snakes goaltender. Before you knew it, both benches were already clearing to go to their respected locker rooms. It was like seeing a lumber yard hit by a tornado as all the players grabbed another in a lock hug ready and waiting for a full fisticuff fight to break loose. The fans were all standing and yelling. It was the first time the whole game that they actually had something to cheer for.

Two of the Blast players were holding on to one Snakes player, both outsized him. They started shoving him viciously. This was the leading scorer for the snakes, a five-foot-nine, one-hundred-and-fifty-pound left winger from Moose Jaw in western Canada. From out of nowhere, Trevor Hatch raced over to protect him slamming both players to the ice and started hammering away. All the players on the ice raced over as a full melee erupted.

The fans were going crazy, even the ticket takers in the concession area ran into the stands to see what all the ruckus what about. The fights lasted about nine minutes before things came to an end. Players were escorted off one by one by the linesman. The Saginaw players were exciting the ice and above their exit way was a handmade sign that stated "Ladies Room." One fan, near the exit way standing near the gate, yelled, "Nice fight, you pussy." The ref had a notepad out flipping page after page writing down his version of penalties.

"Look around you, man, this is old time hockey, baby!" explained Jared, with a big ass grin on his face, arms open to all of the fans.

"They love this shit, it's fuckin' eh…it's wild and this is what hockey fans like to see. Look at them, no one is sitting down, it has everyone's attention."

Kyle looked at him is disbelief. "Yeah and the NHL wants to eliminate this so it would be watching figure skaters with sticks."

After the donnybrook, the Zamboni cleaned the ice during the intermission. In the lobby you heard the fans everywhere talking about it. It's not something you see every game like years ago in minor hockey. But everyone was discussing this in every inch of the arena.

"Snakes penalty to #4, Eric Browstone, five minutes fighting and a ten minute misconduct," said the announcer as everyone was getting back to their seats for the third period. "Saginaw penalty to #16 Wayne Grathe, five minutes fighting and a ten minute misconduct. Snakes penalty to #10 Trevor Hatch, five minutes fighting, two minutes instigating, a gross misconduct and a game misconduct."

The entire arena showed their disbelief and anger of the ref's decision on Hatch. He was the fan favorite, kicked out of the game for sticking up for his teammate who was outnumbered.

"Bullshit, bullshit, bullshit!" the fans were taunting to the ref.

"Get your head out of yer ass, ref!" Jared yelled.

Another man behind him yelled, "I'm blind, I'm deaf, I wanna be a ref!" Some fans went as far as throwing their program and cup onto the ice. The ref went over to the scorekeeper to have him make an announcement that anyone who throws any debris on the ice will be escorted out of the arena.

Kyle yelled to him over the glass, "Get off your fuckin' knees, ref, your blowin' a good game!"

After a few minutes, the Snakes get on the board with a quick wraparound goal!

"Three minutes and thirteen seconds to go regulation, this game is tied at two a piece," Jackson called.

The fans were back into the game as the loud fog horn sounded off after the puck hit the net signaling the audio of the goal. Minutes later another fight broke out…this time a toe-to-toe match between two enforcers. Both players fighting right up against the glass in front of Kyle and Jared. Punches were being exchanged back and forth one after another, both players helmets were knocked off, elbow pads off, and the Snakes player had the Blast players jersey over his head.

"Their arms are locked, he can't do anything, now there's an upper cut!" yelled Jared.

The jersey was pulled right off the Blast enforcer as the linesman separated the two. The Blast player very displeased with the fight, was so upset, yanked the remaining part of his jersey off his arm and threw his jersey against the boards. The glass was not as high in Utica, as most arenas are. The jersey flew over the glass and into the second row of the Snake Pit. Kyle quickly grabbed the jersey as the Blast player went into penalty box, what most dedicated hockey fans refer to as the sin bin. You could see a sign that someone stuck up behind the visiting team sin bin that said, "Ladies Room." Kyle walked a few feet over to the box, where he sat, knocked on the glass to get his attention. He showed him his jersey, then crouched over and took the Saginaw jersey, brought it behind his back and whipped his ass with it, then threw it back over the glass to the shocked player. The fans gave Kyle a standing ovation and was caught on the local 11:00 news.

"The Snakes play-off hopes are slim to none but still a slight flicker of hope as they tied the Saginaw Blast tonight," WUTC News reported. "The Snakes travel to Baltimore, MD, for the next two road games before returning home for their final game of the regular season."

Jared and Kyle watched the news at their local sports bar, Scores. The place was usually close to packed after the games as they offered fifty cent drafts of Dax beer for each goal scored after the games. The bar was a bit larger than average, with benches on the side, instead of your basic pool tables and pin ball machines. They had a small batting cage, a hockey shot net, a basketball hoop, and even a football throw. Many fancy neon beer signs lit up the place with a lot of Dax beer since the local brewery was just a few blocks away.

"It doesn't happen to often but damn, does that pump the fuckin' adrenaline or what?" Kyle asked.

"This calls for a Slap Shot," he proposed.

"Slap Shot" is a jell-O shot that the owner made up. It was a great tasting, cool refreshing, potent bright blue colored jell-O shot that was shaped as a mini hockey puck. He would never give away the secret ingredient but they could taste the Canadian Dr. Migillicutty's in it.

"Gimme a round of the Slap Shot, April!" Kyle yelled to the bar maid. Jared turned to the doorway checking out the sexy, long haired redheaded broad coming into the bar.

"Better make it a double order," Jared said with a grin.

Kyle looked at Jared puzzled. "Gonna be a long night?"

"Fuckin' eh, no, there not for me...for her," Jared explained, nodding his head to the redhead heading their way.

"Hey, doll!" Kyle grinned. "We just ordered some shots, whatya say we have a shot, then I'll give you a shot of my own later on?"

The redhead just looked at him with a conceited look on her face. "Why later on, why not right now, while your friend here can watch and maybe even join in the fun," she replied with a grin.

Jared looked at them shaking his head. "Why don't we just do that, here's a $50 bill that says you don't have the nads," Jared challenged.

The redhead just grinned at him. "$50 wouldn't even give you a wink of an eye."

Sabrina sat down and took her arms and put them around her boyfriend Kyle. They were high school sweethearts and still together today. April brought over the shots to them sitting in the booth, lining them up for them.

"I propose a toast!" Kyle continued. "To the one I have known for about four years now, the one I love dearly," he said as he looked at Sabrina right in the eyes with a gleam.

"Oh, Jesus, no," Jared joked.

Kyle continued. "I owe all my happiness to you, baby, you are my dream come true...I love you...Slap Shot!" he said as he kissed the jell-O shot and downed it.

Jared couldn't even finish the shot without laughing and luckily for Kyle, Sabrina had a good sense of humor about everything. And why not, it's all in good fun. Kyle looks to act like a wolf when out with his buddies but when she is alone with him, he's just a perfect puppy lover.

"Hate to be the spoiler here but I have to split," she sadly said.

"C'mon, hun, you know I'm just kidding, eh?" Kyle asked with his arms open to her.

She hugged him back. "I know you are, sweetie, I'm just tired and have to be into work early tomorrow. The designer is coming in to view my new material I'm proposing for this pattern I've been working on."

"OK, call me when you get home, a lot of nuts on the road at this hour," Kyle ordered.

Jared laughed. "Yeah that's why you need to walk home you lush!"

"Fuck off!" said Kyle as he continued to sip his beer.

Chapter Three: Back to Work

The hockey net alarm clock showed 6:00 a.m. on the LCD display. The radio alarm was going off on the local radio station. "In other scored, the Sabres lost to the Capitals by the score of 3-1, Rangers tied the Bolts 4-all, it was the Sharks pounding the Coyotes 7-2, and on local ice, the Utica Snakes came from behind scoring two late goals to tie the Blast from Saginaw. Unfortunately the Cape Cod Trappers shut out Lansing to take a six point lead over Utica. It isn't looking good for the Snakes right now. In order for them to make the playoffs, they would have to win all three remaining games which the next two are on the road. This would be the fourth time in five years the Snakes would not make the playoffs. We will be meeting with head coach Keller tonight on Hockey Talk."

Kyle was sleeping in his bedroom, a total mess, while Jared's bedroom was across the hall in their two bedroom apartment in a two family home in the native suburb of Whitesboro, NY. Obviously decorated by hockey buffs and sports enthusiasts, the apartment was nice but had collectors and Snakes souvenirs everywhere. Kyle was awakened more by Probert, who was barking at the neighbor's dog along the way. Kyle threw the pillow at Probert, but missed by a long shot. Probert is their dog they named after one of the best fighters in the history of the NHL. Rolling over, he tried focusing at the clock who was still talking sports to him on the AM dial. It displayed 6:36 a.m.

"Son-of-a-bitch!" he shouted, bolting up and darting out of bed.

"Jared, we're late, we're late!" he yelled across the room while trying to get ready.

"Fuck me…I knew we should have gotten a louder alarm clock," he bitched as he hurried into the bathroom with pajama bottoms half off.

"Where the hell are the aspirins?" he yelled to Jared.

Jared yelled back at him from his room, "Probert was whining last night so I figured I would give him something to help him, but don't worry, eh, only gave him two like the directions said, eh."

Kyle opened his bedroom door where Jared was just rollin' out of bed. He poked his head in on that answer he gave him and just rolled his eyes. "In your case, I know you're not joking, get help," he said, closing the door back up.

They threw on their uniforms, grabbed a couple breakfast bars, and darted out the door, into the car. "Dude, tell me you have the keys," Jared asked from the passenger seat, seeing Kyle putting his head on the steering wheel looking at him.

"If I had the keys I would have started the car and been driving, instead of sitting here looking at you ass lick."

In the parking lot of Dax Brewery, Jared and Kyle rushed into work, hurdling the shrubs out front near the door, scanned through to get in and past security.

"Late again, boys?" the security guard asked with a grin. "Can tell there must have been a game again last night."

Jared and Kyle walked into the office area where they had to go through each day to get to the microbiology lab where they worked. Looking all around hoping they would not come across their boss, they stopped by the water cooler against the right wall which was just before the office of Mr. Knapp, their heavyset, miserable, and unsanitized boss. Dana, Mr. Knapp's secretary, was sitting at her desk directly across from Mr. Knapp's doorway working on some papers with her head down. She glanced up to the left corner of her eye, with her hair long and curly, just being able to see through her hair, she noticed the boys standing by the cooler. She looked at them, then peered over to Mr. Knapp's office, then gallantly peered back over to the boys and nodded her head.

Jared looked at Kyle. "Let's break!" he whispered as if they were in a football huddle. They quietly but fast paced snuck past his office.

Mr. Knapp was on the phone with his back turned, never even saw them pass his doorway. Kyle turned to Dana with his thumbs up and winked of thankfulness. Dana smiled and just shook her head and went back to work.

As they headed down the hall to their lab, they passed their mail clerk who they high-fived just like at the games. Inside the lab, the guys were doing their job, testing and experimenting with the hops and barley of the main ingredients of Dax beer, sporting a logo on the right chest of the uniforms they wore. They were gray and blue, the colors for the beer, with black stripes down the side of their pants, almost like a police officer. Their laboratory office had a lot of old Dax beer signs, posters and other items of old replica. Of course the Snake souvenirs were to be seen throughout. The rock music jamming through the big metal screen speakers of their JVC, was basically to void out the sounds of the equipment in use. At least that was the excuse they used so they could rock it out at work.

Jared was reading some numbers off to Kyle while he was measuring the potent added to the test tube. "Igor, get me a couple bat's wings, a goat's testicle and a dong from a horse," Kyle joked as he was pouring tubes together into a stove pot imitating a witch's brew.

"How about Mr. Knapp's tentacles!" Jared joked back.

"Ha-ha-ha, we can't use ingredients that require tweezers," Kyle laughed. "Bring me that box."

"Hey!" the door slammed open as Mr. Knapp yelled. Shocked looks were brought to the faces of the boys. Mr. Knapp, mean-looking and waddling as usual, walked over to the radio to turn it down. "You imbeciles didn't hear the page obviously if your still here," he bitched. "If you kept the radio down to a minimum you would have heard the damn page that Dana made."

"But, Mr. Knapp, it wasn't because of the radio," Jared said, looking as intelligent as he believed he was. "We turned the loud speaker off." Mr. Knapp pointed up his finger and started to make a statement, but then just growled at the confession statement as Kyle kicked Jared in the shin.

"Ouch, you kick like a wuss!" Jared said.

"Oh is that so," Kyle said to him, getting in his face.

"Hockey fight," they both yelled as they started locking each other ready to fight, jokingly around of course.

"Enough of this bull shit!" Knapp yelled, knowing they were only goofing around as they usually do. "I have to be someplace in less than an hour, I need you to deliver this envelope personally to the bank when you leave to go home."

"What? It is the opposite direction from my place," Kyle said, shocked, taking the envelope.

"That's right!" Knapp snickered. "I figured about ten extra minutes should make up your tardy time from this morning... any questions?"

They both looked at each other puzzled. "Not at this time boss," Jared replied, saluting him as a lieutenant.

Mr. Knapp had a real negative opinion on the two clowns. They were immature, obnoxious, and always late. But one thing for sure, they always were good workers that got the work done and then some.

Kyle, hoping to change that opinion, looked at Mr. Knapp. "Hey!" he shouted to Knapp before he walked out. "We have been working on a new project I was hoping you could try?" he asked.

Knapp just looked at him, shaking his head. "This is NOT like the soda flavored beer you came up with is it?" he asked.

"Nope, sir!" Jared said. "This beer is not drinkable!" he said proudly while Kyle went to the fridge to grab their new contraption. He continued, "This beer is not even in a bottle…it's on a stick!" as he pulled it out to show him.

"I pay you guys to quality test the beer, and do measurements, but not be a brew inventor," Knapp said, not even looking at it.

Kyle handed him the beer invention. "This I call a beer-pop!" Mr. Knapp studied it.

"What the hell are you supposed to do with this beer-poop?" he questioned.

Jared looked at him proudly, replying, "You lick it just like a popsicle, kinda gives you a rush and a buzz!"

Mr. Knapp looked at them, looked backed at the popsicle and back at them again with a slight grin. "This could actually be a hot seller, this could actually be something!" he said with a surprise. He then looked them in the eyes. "If we lived in dusks of hell!" he screamed at them. "Get to work god damn it!" He started walking out the door but stopped himself, turned and grabbed the beer-pop and proceeded to walk out the door. "Don't forget the damn envelope," he said, exiting.

Chapter Four: Dinnertime

After work, Kyle went to Sabrina's apartment where she invited him over to have a nice dinner waiting for him. He rang the doorbell. Sabrina had opened the door. Much to Kyle's surprise, she was dressed in a very sexy but imagination filled dress with spaghetti straps. The dress was silver and ran down to the tips of her knees and it was very revealing on the cleavage area.

"I've been waiting for you there hot stuff," she said with a sexy evil grin.

"What has gotten into you?" Kyle asked happily as he entered the door.

She helped him take his jacket off. "I just wanted a nice special dinner for the two of us." Inside the dining room was an immaculate dinner setting, like a high class fancy restaurant. The lights were dim, the music was set, and everything on the table was in place. Even Tippy looked happy sitting under the table. Tippy was Sabrina's brown and white miniature collie, who looked like he could hardly wait for the end of dinner for the table scraps and anything that fell on the floor was fair game for him.

"Why don't you have a seat and I will bring dinner out. I made your favorite," Sabrina said.

Kyle asked, "Prime rib and shrimp?"

"No silly. Okay your other favorite, sirloin steak," she answered.

While she was in the kitchen, preparing for their dinner, Kyle called over Tippy. "OK, boy, we know the drill, right?" he asked the dog as he just looked him in the eyes. "She is not the greatest chef in the universe, so if she messes up the cooking, you know where to go. Just stay here by me," he advised Tippy who was just looking at him with those sad eyes but ears up.

"What?" Kyle asked. "I can't tell her the truth, she tries so hard and I just like her to be happy, is that a sin?"

"Can you be a good gent and light the candles?" she asked. Kyle grabbed the matches on the table and gladly lit the three tiered candle holder on the middle of the table. Tippy just put his head down and put his paws over his eyes. "Thanks for your support," Kyle said while lighting the setting.

She came out with the dinner and placed it in front of him.

"This looks fantastic!" he exclaimed. He was really serious. The steak looked perfect, the potatoes looked mashfully tasty, hell even the squash was the right color this time. They both sat down to eat, right across from each other. As Kyle cut the steak, he noticed what appeared to be ketchup inside the steak. It was not done enough, being mostly red inside. Kyle, being used to this situation, just acted natural and started eating around the edges. After eating most of his dinner, except the middle of the steak, Kyle started secretly tossing pieces of steak to Tippy. Every time she looked the other way, Kyle tossed it over his shoulder, until the last one was off thrown as she almost caught him. He tossed it a bit too high, and landed on top of the curtain of the side window.

"*Ruff, ruff, ruff!*" Tippy started barking, knowing he could not reach it.

"What's the matter, boy?" Sabrina asked, puzzled. She got up and went over to the window…looked at the window and said, "Oh, of all the nerve."

Kyle looked at her in shock. *This is it*, he thought.

Sabrina continued, "We are having such a nice dinner here and now this…well you're not going outside right now, you can wait, now go lay down!"

Kyle just sat back in his chair and gasped a breath of fresh air. Now back to dinner where Kyle just had to finish up that steak not wanting to disappoint her. All of a sudden Kyle got a huge brainstorm. He secretly picked up the cell phone clipped to his waist. When she wasn't looking, he dialed Sabrina's phone number.

"Oh great, another good timing," she said when she heard the phone ring. Sabrina got up to go into the kitchen to answer the phone. Kyle jumped up the minute she left, took a piece of the steak and stuck it to the form, leaned over the table and stuck the steak over the candle to finish off where she left the cooking. Kyle stood the medium rare steak over the fire for about thirty seconds before Sabrina walked back into the room, he quickly sat back down at the chair stuffing the piece of steak into his mouth. He made such a face trying to hide the fact that the steak was incredibly hot and was burning his mouth bad. He quickly grabbed the champagne and downed the glass.

"Such good wine this is!" he replied, trying to stay calm and showing now pain. "This is definitely not a cheap wine by any means."

After dinner, they went into the kitchen to do the dishes. Kyle normally helps her since she does the cooking. "We should get our own apartment one of these days. It would be so much easier," Kyle said.

"You know how I feel about that," she explained. "You know I don't think anyone should live together until they are married. I know it is old-fashioned but that's just what I believe in and you need to respect that…besides you're the one holding up the process," she said, with a questionable grin.

He took her by the hand. "I will propose to you someday, when the time is right, the moment is right and the situation is right," he expressed. "I love you and I will forever in a day."

They kissed happily and went to the dishes. He got the dishwasher set, she was rinsing off the dishes one by one, handing them to him as he would load them into the dishwater. First she handed him a plate, not looking, he just put his hand outward for the next, she handed him a glass, as he loaded that, she handed him another glass, then a cup, then the next this she handed him was not a hard material. It was softer, he looked in his hand and there was Sabrina's bra. He looked up at her, she was standing there topless and smiling, finger extended upward motioning him up. He gladly accepted. He grabbed her passionately and started kissing her all around her neck. It was very intense as his hands ran up and down her shapely body, feeling every inch of her. "I want you now!" she gasped. He took her down the hall, still bodies locked, and brought her into the bedroom, and slammed the door. Tippy's head tilted from left to right, from right to left as he heard them moaning for each other's sexual appetite.

The morning sun was peeking through the blinds, the clothes, all sprawled across the floor, the fuzzy handcuffs visible on the chair next to the bed, the petroleum jelly on the nightstand with the cap off, and the whip cream spray can lying on the top of the bed.

"That was the most erotic thing I have ever done," Sabrina sighed as she rubbed her morning fingers across his forehead.

"I thought you would never go for this but since I knew you were already horny I figured you just might," Kyle said.

She looked at him. "I never even dreamed of having a threesome before," she continued. "You guys were both incredible...and...ohhh, actually he is still down there."

"What?" Kyle asked. He quickly pulled the blankets off of her. *Squeek-ewww* was the sound. Kyle grabbed the blow up doll and shoved him off the bed. "This is my woman!" he claimed. "You had your fun, now get lost before I pop you one!" he said as he tossed him off the bed pounding his rubber face.

Sabrina was laughing away. "What am I ever gonna do with you, Kyle?" she asked.

He looked at her. "Don't ever leave me for an airhead."

Chapter Five: Strike III

The guys met up at Scores. The unique entranceway to where they walked in was like walking into a sports stadium where you had to walk through the turnstiles. They walked to their booth where Sabrina and her friend were already sitting there waiting for them to show.

"These two charming young men are Jared and Kyle. Boys, this is my new friend Renee," Sabrina introduced. "She just started working with us last week."

The boys sat down with them. The Scoreboard was lit up at the center of the bar in the middle of the night club. It was very realistic, showing "Home Team 4, Visitors 0" with two minutes to go in the third period/quarter. In the center of the scoreboard was a nice wide screen TV with ESPN showing the highlights of the games. The rock music was blaring so the TV could not be heard but it did not matter as Jared and Kyle read the bottom of the screen to see what the final scores were and the scoring stats.

"The Islanders got one of the best fighters in the NHL," Jared said while watching a hockey fight on the screen.

Kyle sipped his beer and nodded looking dead center at the TV. "Fuckin' eh, and the Flyers are back in first place again, that's 'cause they have three big heavyweight enforcers on the team."

Jared looked at Kyle. "That is exactly what the Snakes need, eh!" Jared said. "They have all these European players that like the fancy finesse skating, no fighting, and Hatch is the only enforcer on the team and he can't do it all himself."

The guys continued drinking with the girls. Jared browsed up at Renee as she was looking right at him. He quickly looked back down, but found himself not a second later looking back up at her. Not understanding why he did that as he is more of the forward type of guy but for some reason, shyness has plunged him.

She smiled at him.

"So how do you like your new job?" Jared asked.

She smiled more. "It's not bad, still a lot to learn in the fashion industry but I am enjoying it, how about you, what do you do?" she asked, changing the verdict to him.

"I work for the brewery as a mixologist, oh and part-time hockey guru!" he joked.

"Hockey?" she asked. "I love hockey, been playing the game since I was six years old. My father had me in figure skating but I liked the more competitiveness game."

Jared seemed very shocked. "You like hockey?" he asked, overlooking the fact that she even played hockey.

She took the straw out of her mouth in a sexy motion and whispered a bit loudly, "Wanna go one on one, right here, right now...Kyle and Sabrina could watch...right here on the bar...that is if your man enough. Show me what you got, cutie."

Jared dropped his mug that wasn't quite reaching the table. "You're on, baby, but no touching my rod!" he exclaimed.

Ching, ching, the sounds of the quarters dropped into the bubble hockey shaped rod-hockey game near the center of the bar.

"Best of one series, loser buys the rounds for the evening, and I prefer light beers," Renee said as she challenged Jared on the other side of the game.

He looked at her hitting the start button. "Fuckin' eh, you're on!" They were both intensely into the game.

Tied at two all, Kyle yelled over to Jared, "Jar, get over here now!" Jared was too into the game and couldn't take his eyes off it. "Stop what you're doing and get the fuck over here now!" Jared knew this must be extremely serious. He let go of the controls and, *BAM*! Renee just slapped the puck into Jared's net for the winning goal. Jared just looked back and turned his head, heading back to the booth where Sabrina and Kyle were sitting watching the TV above them. Renee was right behind him in deep smile raising her arms up as a champion. Kyle got up and stood on the booth to reach the TV, turned the volume up to hear the news.

"They just said the Snakes players are holding out," Kyle cried out. "April, turn down the music. Please," Jared yelled, begging to the bartender.

WUTC news reported while showing the Snakes logo behind the newscaster: "The Snakes rumors of being financially strapped have come out of hibernation now. The players announced today that they will not play the last two games including tonight on the road and tomorrow's final home game at the Utica Arena." He continued, "The players have come forth to the public for help. Owner Jacques Probst apparently has not paid the players rental leasing nor their weekly pay in several weeks. The Federal Hockey League officials would not comment at this time but can assure fans, the game would not be canceled."

Hatch then appeared on the TV screen in a baseball cap and street clothes. "This is an awful situation. We hope the fans will understand. We love playing the game and more importantly, eh, we love playing in front of our fans, but some of our players are being locked out of their apartments and some of us have little money for food, eh. In all due respect to the fans, we are not going to play on home ice tomorrow, instead we will be picketing for paychecks in front of the arena, eh, and we hope our fans will support us…no other comments at this time, thank you," Hatch said as he walked away from the camera ready to tear.

This has gotten the attention of most of the patrons at the bar at this time. Jared and Kyle just looked at the TV with their jaws dropped to the table, as if the Jaws of Life just opened them wider. They looked at each other. "What the fuck," they said to one other.

The next night the Snakes were scheduled to play the New Haven Hornets. As the Snakes final home game was coming up in just hours, the usual "Fan Appreciation Night" was one of the very few games that sells out. The 6:00 news reported that the game will go on as scheduled, only will be replaced by "replacement" players. The parking lot was filling up by 6:30. The fans were piling up and just about every local TV and radio station and newspaper reporter was on hand. It was more or less to witness the strike than the hockey game.

Kyle and Jared pulled up into the parking lot, unlike the usual times, with their flag out the sun roof, the radio blaring and their air horn sounding off. They couldn't believe their eyes. In the parking lot, the fans were still having their basic tailgate party cookouts but it seemed a lot calmer than usual. In the front of the doors picketing were the players holding up signs. They were dressed in regular street clothes, talking with fans, waving to people that honked their horns as they drove by. It was just a scene like ordinary factory workers on strike. The police station being right across the street from the arena was on high alert in case of any problems presenting. There were two police cars parked alongside the road with their lights flashing.

Jared and Kyle were torn between supporting the organization and supporting the players just like the rest of the 3,000 plus fans that have showed up. They were not sure what to do. The players weren't getting paid. They were outraged. The organization, on the other hand, was in jeopardy and needed all the financial support before they end up folding or going belly up.

Jared and Kyle visited some of the players to show their support before they went around to the side doors to go inside. "Wow…this is like a fuckin' ghost rink in here," Kyle said.

The rink lights were only half on, the players were on the ice warming up only they were not the players they knew. They were "Snake Imposters." They were wearing Snakes jerseys with the players names ripped off the back. If you look carefully you could even see the threading hanging down to wear the name plates were previously attached. These imposter players, referred to as the replacement players were picked up just hours ago by team owner Probst who picked them from local colleges and other teams that have recently dropped players. In the seats, only a hand full of people were there. Those handful of people you could divide them into one person per section and total them up. The players lined up for the national anthem. The Snake Pit section was almost empty but there stood Kyle and Jared. During the song, you could see the replacement players looking up all over the arena. Most of them obviously never played in front of a crowd before. The goaltender wore the old-fashioned brown colored goalie pads. Looked like something from the 1940s.

During the game the crowd was quiet. Nothing to really cheer for knowing the team was gonna either fold or move out of town and the "real" players were left outside picketing in the chilly night air.

By the second period it was an absolute disgrace. The Hornets were clobbering the Snakes, 17-1. The only goal scored was in the first period on a cheap deflection off the boards. Their lone goal did not even get many cheers either. You could see the New Haven players shaking their heads and laughing. Their coach pulled a joke in the third period. With five minutes left, being ahead 24-1, they pulled their goaltender. The Snakes coach complained to the ref saying he was mocking the organization in front of their home crowd.

"This is god damn ridiculous!" Keller yelled. "They have already won the game, why pull the fuckin' tender?"

After the next play coach Keller continued to yell at the ref. The official blew his whistle, skated over to the Snakes bench to warm Keller. "They have every right, they are not breaking any rules and besides, they didn't even put an extra man out," he exclaimed as he laughed skating away. Keller just stood there with a dumb look on his face in a bit of a shock.

Chapter Six: Lotto Numbers

Another ordinary day at work. Jared and Kyle were heading to the break room of the brewery for lunch. Jared stopped by the newspaper machine to get the paper. Jared slapped the chest of Kyle to stop him just as he was stuffing a Twinkie into his face. "Oh shit!" Jared yelled. "That's gotta be a fuckin' misprint."

Kyle looked at him with a disgraced look on his face. "Son of a bitch!" they said in sequence. The *Utica Post*, the local newspaper, front-page headline stated: "Snakes File Chapter 7, Suspend Operations." A photo of an empty arena on one side, and the Snakes front office door on the other with a padlock on it.

"I can't imagine life without minor league hockey, eh?" Jared said.

In Jared's mind, he could see himself switching sports and cheering for the local baseball team. Bottom of the third inning, Utica batter is up, visiting team's third baseman standing near the fence ready for the ball, Jared stands up yelling at him, "Hey, putz, slouched over liked that...your outfielder is checking you out, man." Visiting team pitcher throws the ball and hits the batter, Kyle yells, "Clear the benches...or dugouts, what ever the fuck they are...we want a dawny-brook, hit 'em!"

No, that just wouldn't be the same. Kyle pictured himself too switching sports. The local basketball team had some pep to them. Utica opponents up for a foul shot, Kyle sitting right behind the basket in the front row holding up a poster size picture of Halle Berry in a swimsuit. He had the poster right in front of him like he was pumping her with his love gun from behind. Getting confused during halftime, Kyle turning to Jared. "Where the hell is the Zamboni?" he yelled.

Kyle looked at him is disbelief. "They play on wood, you dumbass, they don't use a Zamboni. It's a floor cleaning truck I am sure."

The guys just looked at each other shaking their head with eyes wide open. "This is not good, eh," Kyle said. "We need to put our heads together and think of something we can do to save this organization."

"Right," Jared remarked, "but what can we do?"

Jared and Kyle were working in the lab, obviously more bummed than normal, when the clock struck five p.m. It was finally time to leave. Not that there was anyplace special to go. The only good thing was it was pay day! Not that there was anything special to buy either.

"Let's go drown our sorrows at Scores, whatya say?" Jared asked.

Kyle agreed, "Sure, I gotta stop and cash my check first."

"Don't bother, I still have some cash on me," Jared said.

The guys shot straight over to Victory's. They came in, not with their heads up as usual but more moping than ever. They came up to the bar. The owner came over and had already opened two cans of their usual. "Your green is no good tonight, save it," he said, shaking his head with a sad look. They just nodded and went to their booth to sit down.

Just minutes later, Sabrina and Renee popped in. "I had a feeling I knew where you guys would be. I'm really sorry to hear about all this. I just wish there was something I could do," Sabrina said as she sat down with Kyle and put her arms around him. Renee did the same with Jared. They just sat there sipping on their cans of Dax. Even the music at this time was more calm. The bar was brighter than normal because usually they are there when it's dark out but this time they were there for the happy hour, or as it is, a fucking unhappy hour.

One of the regulars popped over to the table. He was obviously a hockey fan wearing a T-shirt that stated: "Donate to the American Red Cross...Play hockey." He kneeled over the booth behind them and put his arms crossed over the divider to Kyle and friends.

"Buds...this is totally awful," he said. "We should have seen it coming, Probst is a loser, a crook...a snake. He came to this city in debt up to his friggin' head thinking he could use our money to bail his ass out."

The group just sat there, staring at their cans of beer. Renee joked trying to cheer everyone up, not knowing much of anything about the finances of pro sports looked at the guys. "Why don't we put our money together and buy out the team?"

Jared just looked at her. "Yeah that would work, eh, I heard this just the other day that there was a minor league franchise up for sale! Just two million down, with no financing for one full year!"

Kyle glanced up at the annoying sign about twenty feet in front of him. It was flickering as if it were going out. Kyle stood up as if he had scene the light. He was just staring ahead at the flickering sign.

"Kyle, what the hell are you doing now?" Sabrina said, looking behind her to see what he was looking at.

"Kyle, man, snap out of it, come back to our planet," Jared said.

Kyle stared at the flickering sign. "No shit!" he said. "That is it, that is fuckin' real!" Kyle said. He jumped over the table and ran to the flickering, annoying sign and pointed to it. The sign said: *NY State Lotto*. Displaying it like Vanna White did to the letters, he did to the numbers under the sign. He ran back over to the table.

"Jared, let me see your paycheck," Kyle shouted.

"What for? Why would—" Jared was interrupted.

"Just let me see the damn check, eh," Kyle demanded. "$485, that's perfect!" "But wait, man, how are you making more than me?" he asked.

Before Jared could get a word in, Kyle grabbed his coat. "That's besides the point, let's go." He grabbed Jared and they took off out of the bar.

"Do you mind telling me what the fuck is going on in your head, what the hell are you doing, what is the deal…speak damn it!" Jared demanded.

Kyle made Jared sign his paycheck. Explaining to him what was on his corrupted mind. "That sign in the bar was calling to us," Kyle said.

"It's too ironic, don't you think?" Jared answered and smiled.

"A little too ironic." Jared was on the same corrupted path of mind as Kyle now.

"The team suspending operations, the sign flickering like a firefly, and…and hey, Snakes eat flies, eh, and you and I total over $700 which is lucky #7, this is fate at its best, man. We gotta be destined to win the millions, with $700, that's 1,400 games we got a chance of winning!"

Jared just looked at him in confusion. "You are saying that we need to spend our entire hard earned pay check for the week just to get a one in a million chance of winning millions?" Before Kyle could answer. "Fuckin' eh!" Jared said, putting his fist in the air for the traditional fist slap and high five they do.

"Fuckin' eh!" they both cheered.

They whizzed their car into the parking lot of the 24-hour Quik Stop. They got out of the car and into the shop, cash in hand and dashed to the cashier.

"We need quick pick numbers, we need $700 worth of lotto for tomorrow night's drawing," Jared said proudly. The clerk looked at them like they were pranksters playing a trick or something. The clerk, very big, brawny, and dark-skinned, had a tattoo of a snake-like creature tattooed wrapping around both arms.

"That is a wild lookin' snake, eh," Jared said. "Do you go to the Snakes games?" he asked. The clerk just grimaced at them barely saying a word. "That's OK, man, you don't have to admit it," Jared joked. The clerk just ignored and started punching in the numbers and running the tickets.

Kyle looked at Jared. "Hey let's go get a couple cases to help celebrate." They darted for the beverages high fisting again. Jared, happy as can be, felt infamous as he got the beer out of the cooler and shut the glass door.

Kyle looked at him. "Bud, get the other beer, this is for party pleasure." Jared looked at him and turned back to put the case back in the cooler, forgetting the glass door was already closed and slammed the case into the glass door and...*whhaaak*! The glass door shattered all over the cooler and floor, with a loud hard shatter. Kyle and Jared just looked at each other, looked at the mess, then looked up at the register on the other side of the store straight ahead. The clerk just watched the lotto machine print out the tickets. His radio behind the counter playing hip hop music, and the machine being so loud that he did not even hear the glass break. Jared looked back at Kyle, stepping back while crackling on the glass on the floor.

"We just stick with this case, whatya think?" Kyle nodded as they walked away like nothing happened but a shocked and scared look on their faces. They walked slowly to the counter where the tickets were still being printed. The clerk looking at them from above his register stand, the lotto tickets being printed between them. Kyle and Jared were just waiting for him to say something. He never did. All three just watched the rest of the tickets being printed. Finally it stopped.

The clerk looked at them. "That will be $718. You got ID for the brew?"

The guys looked at each other and smiled. "We sure do, my friend!" Kyle said with pleasure, knowing for sure now that the clerk never realized what had happened.

The boys walked back out of the store and into the car, with their case of beer and a cigar box full of 700 lotto tickets.

Saturday night was a big night. They decided to have a house party at Kyle and Jared's apartment. Sabrina and Renee brought pizza and a couple bottles of Champagne over. They sat down at the table and got out the cards and played blackjack.

"What do you say we have a toast for good luck?" Sabrina said. She got up and poured four glasses of white sparkling wine she put in the fridge. She brought in the drinks, and set them down. They all stood up next to each other.

Renee looked at them with a serious look. "Now please, what ever you do, don't get down if you don't win. Your chances are way too slim to win, life will go on regardless."

Kyle winked at her and then claimed the toast: "Here is to our frame and fortune of having each other as friends, and hopefully here is to another fame and fortune of the millions of dollars that are going to be drawn tonight. The millions that would be considered theirs until tomorrow when it is ours!"

They all smiled and toasted to luck. Sabrina and Renee took a sip to their toast of Champagne, put their glasses down and looked at the boys, who were still drinking, as they downed their Champagne like they were shot gunning a beer, since they were not used to drinking the more expensive beverages. They looked at the girls as they finished.

"What?" Jared asked.

The girls just laughed as they sat down to play cards. They talked about what they would do the whole night, with the millions they could win. The boys wanted nothing more than to run their own hockey franchise. Run it their way.

"Old school hockey, that's what everyone wants. Get a cool name, jersey, and no player under two hundred pounds," Kyle said.

Sabrina explained, "We could have a beautiful house with my own designing room, and indoor pool and a wonderful husband with his dog Probert," she grinned, looking at Kyle who quickly replied.

"No doubt, that's what I would like to, but I don't really want a husband though," he joked.

The evening news came on.

"WUTC News now brings you the New York State Weekend Lottery, operated by Tammy McVie, our lovely lotto assistant," the newsman reported.

She announced, "Thank you, and you're winning lotto numbers are…7…41…31…11…17…and 44. The supplementary number is 22. Thank you for watching and best of luck to all."

Kyle jumped into the air. "We won it, we won, fuckin' eh we won!"

Jared looked at him. "Bud, how do you know we won, eh, we have over a thousand tickets to go through."

Kyle looked at him standing high on the couch. "I can feel it baby, I know it, I just know it, see…the first number drawn is seven…let's find that winning ticket." They all laughed and ran to the kitchen table and started peddling through the numbers.

"One down, two down, three down, three hundred down," they were saying. Their faces quickly going from happy and exciting, to nervous and upset. The night was lingering, getting into the early hours of the morning. Beverages were almost gone, but worst of all the tickets were almost gone. Not too many left to check. The pile at the right end of the table was much taller than the left side, which were the only tickets left to check.

Shaking their heads in disgrace not finding the winning ticket, with about three games left to check, Jared shouted, "I knew I would find the winner," putting his ticket high in the air.

"Let me see that," Renee said. "One, two, three, there are only four numbers here," she explained as the other two just shook their heads in disgrace not finding the winning ticket.

"You're right, Renee," Jared continued, "but that at least means we won a little bit, usually with four numbers we win about $40 or $80!" he reminded them. They all looked worn, their glasses were bare, their pockets were bare, and, worst of all, the table was bare. There were no more tickets to look through. They had lost everything they made for a week.

"This is not fucking happening, shit," Jared yelled. "Search again, damn it, this is supposed to be our night." He panicked looking through the tickets again and again.

"Forget it," Sabrina said. "We lost, that's it, time to move on, Jared." Kyle just watched with his head leaning against the wall.

The next week was really tough. The boys knew they had spent too much for nothing. Now they had no money for the next week for food, or anything. They just had really hard times. The girls did everything they could to help them out. Friday night after work they all went to Scores happy hour again. They ordered pizza and wings. They brought a pitcher of soda over to their booth. Coach Keller came into the tavern shortly after, knowing that the fans usually hang out there. He got a beer and turned and seen the gang over at the booth.

Kyle looked over. "Hey, coach, come join us." Keller grabbed a seat near them and sat down with his arms over the back of the chair. The coach was dressed in just a T-shirt and jeans, something he very seldom wears. In fact the only time they see him, he is either in a suit and tie or a jump suit with skate and stick.

Jared looked at him a bit in surprise. "I thought you would be out of this city by now."

The coach, being a big guy with a humorous attitude, just looked at the group. "When you become my age, and a losing coach, spend your whole life working in hockey, your wife leaves you because of the time you have to spend on the bench, you would know what it is like. I'm not going anyplace now, I have gotten so used to this city, the people here are great and there is a lot of history and potential here, I just don't know where I will go, may just open my own retirement home here someday," he stated.

"You could always be picked up by another team, there are many teams around and many leagues too," Jared said to Keller with encouragement.

The coach just smiled while grabbing his beer. "I have had my share, but the last two seasons have been losing years, not too many teams out there want to hire an old losing coach."

Sabrina, not knowing all that much in the hockey world, felt she needed a woman's voice in this conversation. "Your team was on a low budget anyway, that's the only reason your team was losing, that's why the owner traded away a lot of your good players. You had third line Federal League players on your whole roster."

The coach tipped his glass. "You are very correct, my dear, but unfortunately I'm about ready to retire in another year or two...maybe this is a sign, eh?" The coach continued, "I used to play in this league over twenty years ago for the Hyannisport Presidents. A lot has changed since then."

After the bar, they left to go back to Jared's apartment to watch the Stanley Cup Finals on NBC. After the game, they decided to play a game of Win, Loose or Draw. They set up boys versus girls. After the girls, it was the boys' turn.

Sabrina showed Jared secretly what to draw. He just shook his head and laughed. Jared stuck up three fingers.

"Three words!" Kyle said. First word, Jared drew an eye ball. "Eye?" Jared nodded. Second word, Jared drew a pair of lips. Kyle looked puzzled. "Mouth, um, teeth...lips, um, pucker, kiss..." Jared nodded. Third word...

"Wait a minute!" Sabrina shouted. "This isn't what I wrote."

She was interrupted, Jared said, "No, no, no interruptions...let me finish." Sabrina just sat back knowing that they were now cheating. Jared drew his third and final word. He drew an arrow pointing to the left.

"Arrow?" Kyle yelled. "Ummm, pointer, spot?" Jared stopped. He put his marker down, took the big sketch board and lifted it up, brought it over to the girls and pointed the arrow straight at Renee.

Sabrina covered her mouth. "Oh my god...you want to kiss Renee?" Jared nodded with a grin. Renee was in shock and noticeably blushing.

"If I may?" he asked, putting out his hand.

She stood up and looked at him. "You may." Willingly accepting his lips against hers. They were boldly locked together for quite a long passionate kiss, falling on the couch still locked tight. He was practically on top of her when he finally pulled away for a breather.

"How long have you wanted to do that?" Renee asked him.

He smiled. "Probably a little bit longer than you have wanted to," he said, touching her nose and smiling.

Sabrina giggled. "Well, we will leave you two lovebirds alone…c'mon, lover boy," she said, pulling Kyle by the hand to lead him into the bedroom.

Kyle turned to Jared. "Fuckin' eh!" he said as they high fisted again.

The light was gleaming into the bedroom through the shades. You could hear the birds chirping outside. The morning light, starting to shine onto Sabrina's head, who was sleeping soundly on Kyle's chest. *Ding…dong, ding…dong*, the doorbell rang. The morning hangover has kicked in, Kyle's eyes were just opening, trying to focus on what the hell that noise is. *Ding…dong*, again it sounded. Finally realizing what it was, Kyle got up, with just his underwear on.

Sabrina awoke. "Who can that be this early?" she asked.

Kyle looked at the clock. "It's eleven in the morning, it can't be the pizza guy." He quickly jumped into his jeans to go answer the door. Walking into the living room area, Jared and Renee, practically in the same spot as last night and still fully clothed, were just waking up. Kyle peeked out the window. It was a police car outside in the driveway. He quickly raced over to Jared tripping over a couple beer cans.

"Jared, snap out of it, man…what the fuck did you do last night?" Kyle asked, shaking him to wake up.

"What, what?" he replied, now fully awake.

Kyle looked at him in the eyes. "The fuckin' cops are here."

Jared looked at Renee who had just woken up. "Hey, you are twenty-five, aren't you?" Jared asked her.

She just rolled her eyes. *Knock knock*, the police were not banging on the door.

Kyle and Jared both went to the door. "Who is it?" Jared asked. Kyle slapped him on the side of the head thinking how stupid that just sounded.

"UPD! We'd like to have a word with you please," the officer said through the door. UPD stood for Utica Police Department. They opened the door. There stood a police officer and another gentleman with a badge and a polo shirt and khaki pants.

"This is Officer Mitchell and I am Investigator Harrison," he said. "We would like to ask you a few questions...will only take a minute."

Jared looked at him. "Who was murdered, how many?"

The officer looked at him. "No one was murdered, son, but you guys I presume are Kyle Tucker and Jared Miller?" he asked.

They just looked at each other in shock. "Yes," they both gulped.

The officers looked at each other, then looked back at the boys. "A week ago Friday night, you guys were at the Quik Stop."

Jared looked up. "I don't remember what night it was really."

Officer Mitchell advised, "The video surveillance cameras say you were there on Friday early evening, both of you...anyway, we need you to come down to the police station with us, we will provide you with a ride, since the smell of alcohol is still noticeable."

Sabrina then walked to the doorway. "What is going on here?" she asked still in her nightgown, peeking over the guys' shoulders.

"Please get some clothes on and come with us," Harrison said.

Jared shut the door slowly. "We will be right out, Officer."

Jared quick grabbed Kyle by both arms. "Fuck I knew it," he said.

Kyle asked with confusion "What, what?"

Jared looked him in the eyes. "That fuckin' glass we broke, the store in pressing charges against us."

Renee looked at them oddly. "Do you mind telling us what the hell is going on?" she demanded.

"We busted a sheet of glass at the store last week, looks like we are going to get questioned," Jared claimed.

"So didn't you just pay for it?" she questioned.

"Pay for what?" Jared continued, "We didn't even tell anyone, nobody seen or heard it."

The guys grabbed their jackets and left out the door. "We'll be back in a few," Jared said, knowing it may be a bit longer than just a few.

Walking to the police car, Kyle whispered to Jared, "Remember what any sensible lawyer would say...you don't admit to anything without an attorney present."

At the station the guys followed the officers upstairs. It was a newer police station just built a few years ago. They were led into the other room with a table and a few chairs. The mirrored wall to their left made them all the more nervous.

"Have a seat," Mitchell said while he was sitting himself.

Another office came in with a TV on a stand and a DVD recorder.

"This is the footage we were referring to, please take a look for yourselves," the officer said. They watched themselves on the tube very closely as they walked into the store and went up to the big well-built store clerk who helped them. They realized how they had been caught, wearing their work uniforms from the brewery with their names on a patch on the front of them.

The officer turned it off and said, "That was you two that proceeded in this video, correct?"

The boys looked at each other, knowing they had been totally busted and lying would only get them in deeper trouble. "Look," Kyle said. "It was just an accident, it's not like we intentionally did this and left the scene of a major crime."

The officer looked puzzled and asked, "Oh no?" He leaned over to the intercom. "Please send in Mr. Spanto now." The boys just gulped as they waited to see who was gonna walk in from behind that mirror.

The door opened, in walked a man, about six feet tall, very professional looking with a suit and tie. He was holding a small dark CD box cover.

"You I presume are Kyle Tucker and Jared Miller, I need to see some proper identification of the both of you please," he verified. The boys were speechless. "I am Mr. Spanto and I am here to show you something that you may not be aware of." Mr. Spanto continued, "Please watch this carefully, what we have on video." As Spanto inserted the disc into the player, the video showed the second half of what the officer was previously showing. "As you can see," Mr. Spanto said, "you two walked away from the counter. Here the store clerk's printing out your tickets." He pointed to the screen. "Watch carefully as we switch camera angles…there he is stuffing what appears to be lotto tickets into a small pouch under the counter, now you see him putting yours away." He shut the video off and looked at the guys who looked well beyond puzzled. They were white as ghosts not knowing what was happening.

Mr. Spanto looked at them. "Willy Barnes, alias, the store clerk, has stolen approximately thirty of your lotto tickets. Knowing that you guys would not notice until later, if not at all, he could get away with it because you bought such a mass quantity," Mr. Spanto said.

Jared looked at him. "I don't understand, eh, if he did something bad, why are we in trouble, we had nothing to do with it."

Mr. Spanto just kind of grinned at him. "My friends, you guys are not in any trouble, but we do have the confirmed proof now, and I believe this is rightfully yours," Mr. Spanto said, handing them a shiny gold business card box. "Go ahead and open it," he said.

Jared opened the box with Kyle peering over, there lay a NY State Lotto ticket that had a printing on it that said: "Winner! $8,000,000.00." Underneath were the winning numbers that Kyle and Jared had quick picked on Friday night. "On behalf of the NY State Lottery…congratulations!" Mr. Spanto said with a smile.

Jared and Kyle again were totally speechless. Kyle looked at Jared. "Fuckin' eh!" he said.

"Fuckin' eh!" Jared said back as they just hugged and embraced each other with signs of tears of joy in their eyes.

Kyle and Jared were so happy they didn't know what to do first. Kyle asked to use the officer's phone.

"Watch this!" he told Jared. He picked up the phone, started dialing, waited while the phone was ringing.

"Hello?" answered the frantic voice on the other end.

"Sabrina!" Kyle said. "I'm so glad you answered."

Sabrina interrupted, "Where are you?"

Kyle continued. "I am still at the police station. I can only make one call."

Sabrina interrupted again this time in tears. "Oh my god, Kyle, what did you do?"

"You and Renee need to come down here right away. I'll explain things when you get here," he said, sounding very frantic and in trouble.

The girls arrived there just minutes after the phone call. She ran over to the guys who were standing near a vending machine with their hands behind their back like they were in handcuffs. The girls just grabbed and hugged them.

"What is going on?" Renee asked frantically.

They boys just wrapped their arms around their ladies, surprising them that they were not in cuffs. They quickly backed away. Kyle and Jared high fisted each other facing back to back with handcuffs on as a joke. "You two are dating millionaires, baby!" Jared said.

Kyle interrupted. "That's right, long story but we ended up winning the lotto from last Friday...look!" He had the officer unlock the handcuffs. He showed them the gold plated lip cover and the winning ticket.

The next day, at the WUTC News station, the boys were ready to make a press conference announcement put on by NY State lotto. Local news stations, radio and newspaper were there as well as a crowd of their friends and family. The news traveled faster than light as nothing like this has ever happened locally before.

"Ladies and gentlemen," Mr. Spanto announced while offering them the giant check. "I would like to introduce to you the new extraordinary gentlemen that won the NY State Lotto of eight million dollars...Kyle Tucker and Jared Miller."

They came up onto the podium dressed in everyday clothes, and their Snakes jerseys. "I don't know what the hell to say," Jared said, "other than what I have said one hundred times already," as he put his fist in the air and yelled, "woooahhh!"

The crowd cheered him on. One of the reporters yelled, "How did you pick the numbers, were they your lucky numbers?"

"Fuckin' eh they were lucky!" Kyle slipped, so excited forgetting it was on the local news. "Oops, sorry, um, anyway, we picked quick pick numbers but I see my number zero showed up a couple times!" he said, turning around pointing to the back of his jersey.

Another reporter yelled, "What will you guys do with all this money?"

Jared said, "Well if it is OK with Jacques, we would like to buy the team from him."

"Who is Jacques? Can you be more specific?" a reporter asked.

"Sure!" Jared said, grabbing the microphone. "Yeah, you know, the moron Jacques Probst, the one that owns the Snakes Hockey Club that used our city to pay his debts by butchering a hockey franchise that we had for years. We wanna buy the team from his cheap ass and run it our way, old school hockey way!" The crowd just snickered. Realizing they weren't laughing.

"Anyway, we have work to do, thanks for coming out, eh!" Jared said. "And thank you, NY State!" he added. They walked off the podium.

"They aren't takin' us serious, are they?" Kyle said. "Come on, we'll show them!"

Chapter Seven: Bye-Bye, Snakes

Jared and Kyle went to the local diner for breakfast. They ordered some lumberjack.

"The sale is now official," Kyle's lawyer said while standing at the table between the two parties. "Jared Miller and Kyle Tucker are now the official owners of the Utica Snakes Hockey Club and will be known as partner shares in a LLC Corporation.

Kyle looked at the former owner, Mr. Probst, and shook his hand. "Again I am sorry for calling you a moron and all yesterday."

Mr. Probst smiled and shook back. "That's quite all right, my boy, it was worth the millions," he thanked.

Jared looked at Probst. "Now get the fuck out of our office before we haul your ass out ourselves."

Kyle turned around to Sabrina. "Thanks for your dad helping us with the legal issues," he said.

Her dad had been a lawyer for the last fifteen years and knew the art of buying commercial estates and businesses.

Later that day, the group sat at that the table. "OK, we now own the team," Jared said, "now what the hell do we do from here?"

"First thing we need to do is change that horrid name!" Kyle said.

"It reminds me of what a fuckin' snake that bastard really was, eh," Jared replied.

"That is true but at the same time, I like the concept of a snake, and animal that is. We also should use a name that no one else has." The group just looked puzzled.

"Pythons!" Jared yelled out. All three looked up at him.

"Holy shit, dude…where the fuck did you come up with that?" Kyle asked, surprised.

Jared showed him his key chain of his car starter, it said Python Systems. They smiled knowing it was that easy to decide on a cool name for a sports franchise. "I have an idea!" Sabrina said. "Why don't you let me and Renee work on designing some cool fashionable jerseys?" she asked.

Kyle looked at her and stood up. "Oh, no…I don't want some pink polka dotted players skating around in stockings."

"I'm serious," she said. "This is my job and my life, I would love to help."

"OK, you got to it," he said, giving in with the trust he has for her.

"Now the biggest problem we face yet," Kyle said, walking over to the bookshelf. He pulled out a yearbook of the team, put it on the table.

"Bringin' back the old school hockey," he said. "Let's start weeding out the players that suck, and bring in the players that bring in the luck," he said proudly with a smile.

Jared looked through it. "First players to cut, anyone with less than fifty penalty minutes!" he said as the guys smiled and high fisted again with the fist slap and high five tradition.

"Fuckin' eh," they claimed.

Kyle looked back at the roster. "OK second, any player with names ending in the letters 'OV.'" Again the high fist and fuckin' eh appeared.

Jared grabbed a pen. "Bye-bye, Slakov. Bye-bye, Laginov!" he said jokingly while crossing out the names. The boys started researching other teams. Studying their statistics, looking at videos of other teams and writing down as much information as they could. Going to every game for the past decade, they know most of the players and their playing abilities. The guys sketched up some new players for this idea of bringing back the old school hockey. They decided to get a team of mostly all enforcers. Players that could play the game, make good plays and ones that knew how to put the puck in the net. But most importantly in their minds were never afraid to drop the gloves.

Meanwhile, the *Utica Post* newspaper headlined for the next week about the new team owners. "Team owned by Rookies" and "New Owners, No Comments" headlined. The media was starting to bash the new owners. For one, they had no experience of running any kind of business whatsoever, and two, they would not comment to the media on anything at this time, including the changing of the team name which made the media a bit more leery of what was going on. There were even rumors of the team moving to the Florida Keys and they were building a new arena.

The guys put a stop to that. A week later they called a public press conference announcement was to be made. They also cordially invited all hockey fans and press media to the arena. They said the announcement was so huge that they would have to have it in the arena instead of the typical press room.

The month after, early evening, people started lining up at the front doors of the arena. It was a dark warm night. Four big blue laser lights flashed up in the sky back and forth from the arena. The front door marquee said: "Hockey Open House Tonight."

As the fans came, more out of curiosity than anything, they walked into the arena to see a huge change. The hockey boards were up, but no ice. At the stage area was a huge odd shaped back ground with a blue tarp over it and a podium. "Welcome Utica Hockey Fans" the sign shined from above. The place started getting extremely packed as the media blew it out of proportion about the team moving, or the owners not knowing what they were doing. Over 2,000 fans showed up for this announcement which was more than the Snakes averaged for a game.

The lights dimmed, the rock music started blaring. It looked like the beginning of an Ozzy Osbourne concert. Jared and Kyle came to the podium. "I want to thank everyone for coming!" they said. "First off we would like to say that the Snakes as you know are now history." The crowd started to yak a bit loudly sounding of concern.

"The team name will be known now as your Utica Pythons Hockey Club!" Kyle said with his fists in the air.

Some of the crowd started cheering...others were reluctant and confused.

"The entire arena will now be known as the Snake Pit! I know you guys wanna know your new team colors, eh...well, they will NOT be that hideous Snake colors!" He pulled the string that released thousands of balloons and confetti from the rafters of the arena. It rained the colors of florescent green, navy blue and black. The crowd started cheering wildly and the party atmosphere erupted and the music went on again as the concert lights were flickering.

"I would now like to introduce to you the players that will be taking the ice next month," Kyle said.

Marc Jackson took over the microphone to introduce the players. "Welcome to the Snake Pit, Python fans!" the far too familiar voice sounded to the fans. The calm cool radio announcer was now sounding more wild, upbeat and growling. "We would like to introduce your new Utica Python players...

first…ummm…hold the phone for a second," he said and stepped away from the microphone to lean over to Jared. "Is this a joke?" he whispered to him. "What the hell is this?" he asked.

Jared looked at him and said, "Old school hockey!" with his fist up.

Jackson went back to the microphone. "Python fans," he continued, "the following players have been released by the organization…Fraklov, Modin, Lastrov and Baily," Jackson said, sounding more surprised and shocked. The fans started booing since a couple of those were fan favorites of Utica fans. "The Pythons plan to weed out the weak and bring in the strong old school hockey. Introducing your new Pythons starting lineup!" he said as the lights went dim again, and the sparks started shooting out of the stage center background with a big tube hole that the players would come out of. "Your Snakes team leading scorer, and now your Pythons captain…#7 Scott Pyle!" Jackson announced as the crowd cheered him on as he ran out onto the stage with his new Pythons jersey. The fans seemed to love the jersey as you seen a lot of the fans pointing to it. It was nothing like any hockey fan had seen before. It wasn't your basic boring flat color jersey with stripes. It was a neon green and navy blue snake skin all over it with stripes on the upper and lower sleeves and bottom of the body. The mean-looking logo on the front was very large and the numbers on the sleeve and back was very wild italic looking with a snake bite on the bottom right of each number.

"On defense, your fan favorite is back, #10 Trevor Hatch…On wing, from Moose Jaw in Canada, scoring 26 goals and still managing over 200 penalty minutes…#2 Matt Lawless!"

The crowd cheered louder and louder and the excitement was building.

"Born and bread in Brooklyn, in his first pro season, coming in with a heavy weight title and a positive attitude to kick some Federal League ass...#55 Darren Roach...your goaltender for this season, having thirteen years of aerobics and gymnastics and figure skating, along with goaltending, just out of Cornhill High School, #0 Craig Kilroy. Your coach for the Utica Pythons, your favorite is back...Lee Keller!"

The players were lining up in front of center stage and high fisting as they lined up (as taught by Kyle and Jared). They introduced the rest of the players that will be taking the ice, leaving a few spots open as they were not completed yet. They looked more like a football defensive line. They had the size, attitude, grit and a future.

Darren Roach, a rugged black African American player, was definitely a minority in the sport of hockey. But he was cut from several teams because of his attitude antics on the ice after a fight or after scoring a goal. They were all positive but the coaches didn't see that in hockey. That was something football players did in the end zones.

Lawless, on the other hand, looked like something from a Bon Jovi rock band with his long black hair. He was a big brawny wrestler looking guy that skated hard.

Kyle stepped back up to the microphone. "I hope everyone is ready for the Pythons to take a bite out of their opponents this season!" They cheered! Kyle knocked on the microphone. "Hello...I didn't say the Snakes...I said the Pythons...are you ready?" he yelled louder. The fans cheered three times louder. "That's better," he said. "This will be the old school hockey your elders told you about. In case you were wondering, Coach Keller, wearing a player's jersey, will wear it behind the bench, he doesn't need a suit and tie...he is part of the team. The ads on the boards...they didn't have them in the 70s and they won't have them here today. The ice will have a light blue tint to it, to show better sighting of the puck and less light glare from the arena lights. The scoreboard will be replaced with a video replay screen, and we will not go down without a fight…we will go down with a brawl if we have to!" he exclaimed. "Thank you all for coming and we hope to see you in two weeks when we host the Cape Cod Trappers." The crowd again cheered for a minute or two before exiting.

The lights circled all around the Utica Arena with the marquee out front showing, "Pythons Season Opener Tonight." The crowd sold out to capacity of 4,567 standing room only to see and witness what is supposed to be considered the turn of the century for hockey according to the *Utica Post.*

Kyle and Jared, along with Renee and Sabrina, sat in the newly built luxury boxes about the south end of the arena. In the corridor, the fans were piling in. The souvenir stands had lines for merchandise like never seen before in Utica. The fan club booth had people gathered. Fans were buying programs to look at the lineups of these new players. Inside the seating area the people were starting to fill the seats. The dasher boards, instead of companies or corporations, had "Go Pythons" and "Welcome to the Snake Pit." The Pythons logo took up the entire center face-off circle. As they introduced the players coming out of the locker room, they had the lights dim and the spot lights and fireworks show for each starting player. They then announced the coach and the team owners, then announced the "MVP," which stood for Most Valuable Pythons, the Python fans! The players lined up for the face-off. The Trappers are in their green and yellow jerseys.

"We are ready for the first ever face-off in Pythons' history!" Marc Jackson called on the radio. "Scott Pyle will face it off for the Pythons against the Cape Cod Trappers, the ref is ready to drop the puck, and…wait…it looks like winger Matt Lawless is coming into the circle, he is saying something to Pyle…looks like they are switching places." Jackson continued, "Usually you see them switch players on the power play in the opponent's end, but on an opening face-off…and the puck is dropped…ohhh and it looks like so is the Cape Cod forward, ohhh, and another, and another, looks like the triple decker!" Jackson yelled with excitement.

"Five seconds into the game and the excitement has already swung up!"

When the puck was dropped Lawless instead of going for the puck, went for the body and checked hard, immediately after, the two wingers followed through.

Jackson continued, "Pythons defense brings the puck out in control with the puck, skated it into the neutral zone and slap shot the puck into the goal, which was saved by Trappers goaltender Hanna, Pyle skating across the crease, got the puck and backhands it from behind. Score! Just eighteen seconds into the opening season and the Pythons take their first lead."

The other team sent out their goon. He lined up the wing of the face-off circle at center ice, a tough guy that was obviously sent over the bench on a mission.

The goon looked at Lawless. "You pull another stunt like that, prick, and you'll be eating your chipped teeth, got it?" he said.

Lawless just looked into his eyes. "No, maybe you should put that shit in writing and send me an RSVP."

The puck dropped and so are the gloves of Lawless and the Trapper enforcer. They throw fisticuffs back and fourth, with the fans on their feet cheering. Kyle and Jared started to leave their executive box going down the stairs.

Meanwhile, Lawless finished the fight and the linesmen

broke them up. "Thanks for the invitation, sorry it was signed with your own blood though, tough guy," Lawless yelled before being escorted to the sin bin.

The boys head back to their seats, only not in the executive luxury box, but back to the bottom of the Snake Pit section with their buds.

One of their friends they just sat next to looked at him. "Hey, your seats are still open, man, no one sat in them!"

Jared looked at him and showed him two tickets. "That's right, eh, we bought our seats this year again, just like every year!"

"These are the best seats in the house!" Kyle commented, laughing. "You think we would actually have any fun sitting with the execs?"

In the third period, the Pythons were tied at 4-4 with about four minutes to go in regulation.

Keller signals the ref for a time out. He called the players over. He looked at his players, all standing against the boards in a huddle.

"Take this game as a preview," he explained to his troop. "This preview is of the season, the birth of something new, what we do know is what you wanna show our fans, the ones that pay your salary this season. Don't let them down. Now take that fuckin' puck and own it." He picked up a puck on the bench. "It has our logo on it, doesn't it? Doesn't it?" he asked louder and louder.

They all yelled "yeah!" out loud.

Darren Roach, the only black player on the team, yelled to his teammates, "He don't want a 'yeah,'" he said, mimicking. "He wants a 'hell yeah!'" he shouted. "Now gimmie a hell yeah!" The players yelled it loud!

The ref blew the whistle to let them know their timeout was up.

Roach looked up at the coach. "Sorry, coach, just tryin' to get them pumped, no haten!"

The players went to the face-off circle with the coach standing there a bit in shock.

"I'll have to try that sometime," he said, mumbling to himself.

The players lined up at the Trappers end of the ice. Lawless lined up to face-off against the Trapper center for the draw. Lawless looked at him as they bent down, face to face.

"Ever been checked hard right after the puck is dropped?" Lawless asked him looking fierce as ever. The opponent was a smaller five-foot-eleven, one-hundred-and-seventy-pound guy that Lawless could easily crush him hard. The player didn't answer him but instead just put the blade of his stick onto the ice ready for the face-off. You could easily see the fear in his eyes as he tensed up.

The linesman dropped the puck, quickly, the opponent's first reflex was instead of going for the puck, he brought his stick up in fear of being hit by the bulldozing animal. Instead, Lawless went right after the puck and took it like candy from a baby.

"Sorry, sucker!" he yelled as he passed the puck behind him. He had no intention of checking him, just loved to see the fear in other's eyes.

Jackson calls the play by play almost laughing. "Lawless fakes the check and the Trapper is just standing there, Lawless passes the puck to Hatch, feeds forward to Pyle, back to the blue line, feeds Roach in front of the net...he scores! Darren Rooooaaaccch hits the biscuit in the basket!" Roach with the attitude of a football player, ran on his skates up all the way to center ice and started waving his stick like a lasso and fell to his knees sliding about twenty feet before coming to a halt and putting his hands in the air as the players raced over to pat him one. Even the coach cheered with emotions that he never expressed that much before.

The remaining three minutes was just played to kill time. The Trappers pulled their goaltender with a minute remaining. The Pythons goaltender Craig Kilroy made some real aerobic saves. Hatch made sure that no one stood in front of him. They just could not get any solid shots on net.

The Trappers last shot came with about fifteen seconds to go, Kilroy with his goalie mask being mostly wired bars, and not much art work to it, made a major face save. Hatch picked the puck back and shot it very slowly down the length of the ice…took 8 seconds to get there to be precise wish would mean only seven seconds for their team to skate back into their end…time up!

Jackson called the game: "The first game in Pythons' history, Utica beats Cape Cod, and remain unbeaten this season…well I've always wanted to say that!" he said, knowing they are only one game into the season but being the old Snakes broadcaster, they never won their openers before.

Chapter Eight: Utica Pythons

Jared and Kyle went to the local diner for breakfast. They ordered some lumberjack breakfast specials, the waitress asked them if they go to the hockey games, noticing their jerseys.

"We go to them occasionally, depending on my schedule and if it permits me to," Kyle joked.

The waitress looked him. "I haven't gone since I was a little girl. I guess some guys won the lotto and bought this team so I went and I loved it…well, anyway, I'll bring your coffee right out," she said, realizing she was very much babbling.

Kyle and Jared looked at each other and snickered. "That really must be true about those blonde roots eating away at the brain tissue," Jared said. "Nice girl though, eh."

Kyle's mobile phone rang. "Hay-lo," he answered. A brief pause. "OK, hun, we are at the diner, bring him here first." He hung up the phone. "We will be having company for breakfast this morning," Kyle said to Jared who looked very puzzled. But it really didn't seem to faze him as he looked at the local paper seeing the headlines: "Utica Pythons Fighting For Attention."

"I don't understand this, we have sold out three out of our four home games and are unbeaten thus far, what the hell does the media want?" he asked.

Reading the paper to Kyle, Jared read, "'The two boys that won millions that brought the team, Miller (24) and Tucker (26), seem to have brought the fans into the turnstiles, something that hasn't been done in decades locally, but is having a team of mostly heavyweights and enforcers actually helping them win or are they just luck games? The fans seem to love the fighting. With everyone on their feet cheering not only the goals but the fights as well, which makes it more entertaining. The real test will be coming this weekend when the Pythons go on the road for four games. The rumors have all ready circulated around the Federal League that this franchise is nothing but goons and freaks, as claimed by a fan in Lansing, VA.'"

The waitress brought the breakfast plates to them and served them. Shortly after Sabrina and Renee walked in with a man with a backpack. He looked very rugged, had a goatee and a scar over his left eye. They walked over to Kyle and Jared's table.

Sabrina pointed to the guy. "Well, here he is, he was waiting at the bus station and yelling at a janitor there. Anyway this is Boone Davidson, the Windsor, Ontario, player you picked...Boone, this is Mr. Miller and Mr. Tucker, the owners and managers of the Pythons," she said as she stepped a bit behind him showing her finger to her head in a coo-coo motion.

"How the hell are you, my friend?" Kyle said with a mouthful of food, putting out his hand.

Boone just looked at him not putting his hand out, then looked at Sabrina and Renee. "Is this a fucking joke or what?" he asked. "These guys are fuckin' fans, where the hell is the manager?" he demanded.

Jared looked at him. "Mr. Davidson, have a seat, man, really, please." He motioned him to pull up a seat to their booth. Renee grabbed a chair from the table next to them. He hesitated and sat down not taking his eyes of them. Jared pulled out his binder file and opened it.

"Mr. Boone Davidson, suspended from the EHL for disciplinary actions, suspended from the IHL for disorderly conduct and behavioral matters, and the NHL suspended you for aggravated harassment, abuse to an official and disciplinary reasons. You are now playing in a Senior League in the province of Quebec under Canadian probation and you work full time in a tire factory, is that correct?" Jared asked him.

Boone just looked at him, not looking shocked or surprised. "You have done your homework, kid, so what?" he said.

Kyle looked over at him. "You wanna play pro hockey again, you will play for us without the problems, tempers, attitudes or arrests."

Boone looked at him. "I can't guarantee that, man, I am the way I want to be and no one will change me."

Kyle pulled out a $100 bill, took it between his hands and slowly ripped it down the middle.

Boone looked at him with a squinting eye and laughed. "Are you trying to scare me, kid? It won't work."

Kyle put the bill down on the table. "Wanna guess again?"

"OK," Boone said, sitting back in his chair. "Then you are saying that will be my bonus if I behave, eh?" he asked.

Kyle shook his head, looked at Jared and laughed, looked back at Boone. "There are absolutely no bonuses for that, that is part of your pay," he continued as he got up. "Every time you have an outburst like in your past, there will be five of those deducted from each of your paychecks you receive from our organization, and it's all documented in writing here on the contract you can sign if you want to play for us."

Boone sat back again, crossed his arms and shook his head. "I'm not owned by anyone, what makes you think I would sign a contract breached like that, eh?"

Jared looked straight at him bending down to his eye level. "Well it is either you sign that and play for us, or it's just back to the rubber factory and play hockey with the old goats and not ever get paid for playing the game you love again…your choice, my friend," he said as he winked and stood back up.

Boone shook his head. "My mother always said, stay out of hot water, play on ice." He smiled slightly as he grabbed the pen out of Jared's hand. "I want a copy," he claimed.

At Scores, Kyle and Jared walked in with their two ladies by their side. They had their usual Pythons jersey with the same numbers they wore when the Snakes were in existence. All the money and fame wouldn't change anything, they still were the same old hockey fanatics they always have been.

A couple guys came up to them as they sat down in their booth. "You guys are doing an awesome job, five games into the season and unbeaten, who says old school hockey don't win games?" he favored high fiving them. The friendly guy continued, "I just signed up for the Python's Fan Club bus trip going to the Baltimore games weekend, it would be great if your players could give us a signal of appreciation of our support," the fan said. He was in a Pythons dark blue home jersey, with number one on the back and the front where the "C" (for captain) goes, it had an "EH."

Kyle noticed that and acknowledged him. "We will be there to support you guys as you support us, man, and by the way, who are initials are EH?" Kyle asked.

The fan looked at him. "The captain gets the C, the assistant gets the A, but I didn't know what to put there, eh…eh…eh?"

Kyle and Jared looked at each other, they laughed, getting the joke of the Canadian "eh" slang.

Scott Pyle and Darren Roach walked into the club. They went in and sat at the table at the far end. Shortly after about four other players came in. They sat down with the other players. Matt Lawless picked up his mobile phone and made a call. The phone rang behind the bar.

April, the sexy, mature bartender, picked up the phone. "Scores," she answered.

Matt looked right at her. "Yes we need a round of shooters at table four please."

She looked over across the bar, the players were all looking at her and motioning her to them.

"You're a bastard!" she said back on the phone, smiling, knowing that she had been had.

Matt replied, "Hey, give us a round of the Drs and one hot Kamikaze!"

"Sure, who is the lucky sap getting it this time?" she asked.

Matt just smiled. "Line 'em up and surprise us!" The Drs shooters were a very cool mint taste but one shooter was to be a mix of Kamikaze and a touch of Goldshlauger (without the gold). Both shooters were a clear drink. No one could tell the difference until after it's already in your mouth.

April came to the table and claimed good luck to all. "This one is for the road, boys, everyone grab your drink and do not sniff nor taste it till the word go. Go!"

Everyone grabbed their drink. "Once…twice…threes…go-go!" Matt yelled.

The players gulped the drinks. "Ohhhh, oweeeee!" Kilroy said, shaking his head like a dog that just sniffed hot peppers shaking his cheeks back and fourth. "You guys are too fuckin' evil, give me a stinkin' root beer!" he said in his feminine voice.

The guys just laughed hysterically, knowing that he is more than likely gay, and why not, usually the chances of a man that takes aerobics class is at some point.

Meantime, a pizza man walks into the bar with three boxes. "Pizza's here, who's got it?" he yelled.

Pyle stuck his fingers in his mouth and whistled, "That would be table four again, eh!" he said. The guys crowed down on their pizza. They all grabbed the slices by the handfuls.

Moments later a few other players walked into the bar. "The bus is here, guys, let's roll!" one of the players yelled. The players all took one last bite and sip and headed out the door. Some of the fans at the bar area shouted, "Knock 'em dead" and "Bring home the W's!"

As they departed on to the team bus parked out front, Kyle and Jared said goodbye to their ladies. Meanwhile the players boarded the bus.

Kyle grabbed the clipboard. "Bus leaves here in five…we shall arrive in Baltimore by seven a.m. and practice on the ice at 9:30, the weight room at the hotel will be available after practice."

Kyle went over and sat with the coach. He had a box with him. "This is for you, coach, please…open it," Kyle said. "What is this, an early birthday present?" he asked. Kyle shook his head.

Coach Keller opened the box, then opened what appeared to be headphones and a walkman. "What is this?" he asked.

Kyle looked at him. "Put it on," he said. "NFL coaches wear them to help them with their games. I figured why not for hockey. I see it as four eyes are better than one set of eyes. I'll be noticing more from a higher level, if I see any play that needs to be changed, or some out of position. I will call you. I will be able to see the whole ice from above."

The coach just smiled. "I can't keep up with technology but it's a good idea."

Just as they were ready to leave, they heard a voice shouting outside the bus. "Yoo-hoo…guys…yoo-hoo…wait up." It was a guy running up to the bus. The bus driver opened the door. The man was out of breath.

"This is for Craigster, please give this to him," the man said. It was a goalie mask, a real goalie mask, to replace the one that Craig Kilroy wears that looks more like a cage.

Craig overheard and quickly jumped up to get it. He was excited.

Bringing it back to his seat the guys starting mocking him. "Killroy's gotta boyfriend!" they chanted. He just blushed. It was something the players accepted him as and they just have fun with it and luckily Craig has a good sense of humor about it, knowing that they are not against it. He was looking at his new goaltending mask. It was dark blue and black with lime green caged wires. It looked really mean, with a snake's head on each side.

The horn beeped from outside. Headlights were coming straight for their bus parked in front of Scores. As they turned to park next to them, the players could see another bus. It was the Pythons Fan Club bus, they had organized a trip to follow them in Baltimore and New Haven. Their bus parked right next to the players bus, the roof escape hatch opened, out climbed one of the fans, waving a Utica flag! "Let the road trip begin!" he yelled with beer in one hand and flag in the other.

Chapter Nine: Hit the Road

The teams took the ice. The crowd was a capacity sell-out in Baltimore with more people wanting to see this Utica Pythons goon squad just to see what all the hype around the league was about. This was not a team that went out and started fights by any means. This was a team that got under the skin of their opponents. A team that didn't take those stupid cross checking or tripping penalties that would cost the team two minutes each, a team that would not back down from anyone.

The Pythons came out first in their black with blue and lime green snake skinned jerseys. The fans immediately started booing them. Some holding up signs that said, "Go Home Goons" and "Streak Ends Here." After the players skated around their end, the music started playing, the crowd stared to clap as they introduced the starting lineup. The Pythons fan club sitting right behind their bench started chanting "Let's Go Pythons" to try to drown out the crowd. The crowd responded back by booing the fan club. The puck is dropped, Lawless wins the face-off, pulls the puck back to Hatch, passes it just short of two lines over to rookie Tanner LaChance, born and raised in natural ice of Brampton, Ontario, playing junior hockey by age fourteen. LaChance was forced to quit hockey after his parents were deceased from a car accident at age seventeen. He never found the urge to go back on the ice, even after NHL scouts were eyeing him with contracts. Being very close to his family he put off hockey to take care of his younger brother and sister. LaChance was persuaded to come back after his friend, Trevor Hatch, invited him to come watch a Pythons game, that there were good things in the game of hockey that was being done here in Utica. Hatch told him that since his sister is now in college and his brother is now in the military, to come play hockey and don't stay home alone. He demanded this until he gave in.

LaChance received the puck on the pass from Hatch, skates forward, ahead of the defenseman, fakes a slap shot, moves the puck around the other defenseman, just five feet from the net, winds up for the slap shot, but does not shoot it again. The Gulls goaltender falls to the ice on the fake and LaChance very lightly shot the put into the upper right hand corner of the net.

"Scooooooorrreee!" Jackson announced on the radio waves. "His first Federal League goal in just two games for LaChance from a beautiful pass from Hatch, I think the other assist will go to Lawless, and Utica takes the first goal lead!"

The start of the third period, the Gulls started playing more physical. The other new player, the juvenile, Boone Davidson, still sitting the bench, has yet to play a shift. Kyle had told the coach before the game not to skate him yet.

Jared looked at Kyle. "When the fuck are you gonna put in Davidson? You can see he is getting pissed off on the bench."

Kyle looked back at him. "Yeah, I think now is a good time, being ahead by a goal, we need to keep this lead."

Kyle picked up the head set as they sat above in Baltimore's press box. "Hey, coach, take out LeDruce, put in Boone and let's see what he can do."

The coach nodded. "Boone, get your ass out there next shift and show us something to keep you here."

The next shift, Davidson climbed over the boards onto the

ice, he quickly took a pass to the slot, wound up big and took a slap shot. The Gulls goalie never moved, he didn't see the puck, until Boone looked straight down, the puck apparently didn't move either. It just sat there as he fanned on it. He looked up, but it was a second to late as one of the Gulls players leveled him.

"Temper...temper," Jared said softly.

The same player that leveled him had a clear break away grabbing the puck, he skated the length of the ice and from fifteen feet away he took a hard slap shot. Kilroy made a spectacular save in his glove hand as he reached out as far as he could. The player didn't stop skating at him thinking the goaltender would drop the puck, he leveled Kilroy to the ice, hitting the back of his head on the net cross bar.

From out of nowhere, Davidson charged at him and tackled him. "You don't touch my fuckin' teammates like that, you ignorant bastard!" Boone yelled as he totally pummeled him with a dual left hook and a right, back and forth.

The linesman grabbed Davidson, the big ape, off the Gulls player, and escorted them both to the box, when the Gulls player escaped from the linesman and skated after Davidson. The crowd giving a standing ovation over the excitement.

The announced penalties were both teams at even strength and would play the next two minutes with a four on four which meant a lot of open ice. In the penalty box, both players were standing on their feet, having a verbal confrontation at each other, with only a pain of glass, a small time keeper and announcer in the middle of it all. The fans cheered them on but nothing happened. Back on the ice with just four minutes to go, Roach jumps off the bench for a line change. Lawless has the puck on the other end and feeds him the puck. Roach skates behind the net and he had just seconds before he would get hit, he quickly flicked the puck onto the stick blade and tossed it lightly over the net and hitting the goaltender in the back of the head, and the puck trickled down, hit the back of his glove and crossed the line for another goal.

"Yes! Eat that biscuit for breakfast, baby!" he yelled to the goaltender as he skated to the blue line doing the arm pump motion. He looked at the scoreboard; it was now a 3-1 Pythons lead.

Shortly after the next whistle, the enforcers were both let out of the penalty box. Next face-off, both players came out and lined up. The adrenaline was there, everyone knew it and was cheering. Although a bit quieter than the last cheer as the home team was down by two goals. Sure enough, after the puck was dropped, so were the sticks and gloves of the two players for round two.

One of the Gulls players on the ice, did not wanna see his team mate getting this shit beat out of him again like earlier, so he jumped Davidson from behind, that led to all ten skaters on the ice grabbing hold of one another. Then another fight broke out, Lawless was going after another Gulls player. Both fights lasted a good forty-five seconds before it was over. The linesman tossed out four Pythons and four Gulls players. As Boone excited the ice, he passed their goaltender, made a move like he was gonna jump him but he didn't. The goalie ducked and flinched which was actually quite funny in a slick move. Boone went to the locker room and sat on the bench with Lawless who was also kicked out of the game.

Kyle and Jared walked into the locker room to see what the hell happened. "Great fight but what the fuck was that last stint you pulled with their goalie?" Kyle asked.

Boone looked at him all sweaty and reddened from the punches he took. "That was my game plan to make sure we would win the game."

"How the fuck do you figure?" Jared asked him.

The radio was blaring in the Utica locker room, Jackson calls the play: "Score! The Pythons score the insurance goal and it's four to 1 with 40 seconds to go in the game, I don't even think their goaltender saw it coming!"

Davidson looked back at them. "See, that was the plan, to shake their goalie up by scaring the shit out of him, and so it worked, so I will keep my $100, eh!" he smiled.

"Keep it!" Kyle said. "That was a genius plan, I'll give you that much." The Pythons came into the locker room winning yet another game. It was a wild party and they all celebrated the win.

The Pythons arrived in New Haven about three hours before game time. The fans all ready started talking shit yelling at the Python players as they exited the bus to get into the arena. One of the fans yelled at Boone. He started to walk towards them, Kyle opened the bus window right next to him, holding out a $100 bill. "No-no, Mr. Davidson!" he said. Boone just looked back behind him, turned and went into the arena.

Inside the Pythons took the ice. They saw their dedicated fan club sitting right next to their bench. As the game progressed, the fans got louder. They seemed much more obnoxious than in Baltimore. These were very dedicated New Haven Hornets fans. It didn't take long in the second period to break a scoreless tie. The siren went off, the Hornets scored on a rebound, when Kilroy went down. The New Haven crowd started chanting "Pythons suck…Pythons suck…Pythons suck!"

The players were going to the bench for a line change, the Python fan club being right behind their bench started cheering. In the very front row was a Python fan with a sign that read: "Baltimore sucks."

Jared pointed at the fan to Kyle from both sitting high above.

"Oh shit, that kid has a total death wish, fuckin' eh!" he said, looking down at him shaking his head. The crowd booed even louder as a few of the fans behind them started throwing things down at them. Some of the Python fans started throwing stuff back at them. All of a sudden a couple cups of soda and beer were thrown at the fans, only they went over their heads and onto the bench of the Utica players. The backup goaltender sitting on the bench, along with Roach and Davidson, and a couple others stood up on the bench, grabbed the water bottles and started squirting the fans and challenging them to come down closer. The security guards quickly intervened there before it got out of hand.

Jared and Kyle rushed over to help their fans who at most, were soaked with soda and beer. Order was shortly restored as five New Haven fans were escorted out of the building. One of the fans yelling back at Lawless while being escorted out flipped him off. Lawless just laughed and put his stick between his legs and did a stroking motion to him and then waved bye-bye. With just eight seconds left in the period, the ref blew the whistle to end the period. He sent the players to their locker rooms to cool down and relax the fans a bit. They would add on the eight seconds in the next period. The players went into the locker rooms to rest up for the next period.

Coach Keller took a stick and banged it off one of the lights in the ceiling that shattered. "You guys need to fucking wake up, watch the game, and play the game. These fans are animals. They are taking your mind off the game too much. You need to focus out there. I seen barely any checking, fore checking or squeeze plays, hell the power plays aren't even with us tonight."

Kyle walked in. "Keller is right damn it. I brought you guys together for a reason, old school hockey is still a winning tradition. I know you guys are tired from the bus rides, but only twenty minutes left to play, let's finish this game and go back to Utica and get a few days' rest," Kyle said.

The players exited the locker room and returned back to the ice. In the entrance gate to the ice were some fans yelling at them. One fan leaning over the railing calling the Utica players a bunch of "pussies." Davidson stopped dead in his tracks and turned around to look at this guy. The fan quickly backed up and the look of shock stuck on his face.

Davidson turned back around. "I thought so!" he said as he skated onto the ice. "See, you're nothing but a pussy, Davidson!" the fan yelled bravely again, knowing he really couldn't hear him but had to protect his manly reputation behind the glass.

With three minutes left in the game, you could see the team was really starting to get tired. The water bottles were mostly empty and the players were breathing heavy. In the Pythons zone, the Hornets player went to shoot the puck into the corner of the boards. The puck hit directly onto the corner section of the boards where the end piece was sticking out. It took a bad hop as Kilroy went behind the net to stop it. The bad hop bounce deflected back in front of the unguarded net and the New Haven forward slapped it into the empty net. The siren went off. The fans were rocking the place. The scoreboard said 3-1 Hornets lead.

"Call a time out, get them back into the game, feed to the neutral zone harder," Kyle said into the headphones to their coach. Keller motioned to the ref for a time out.

The players gathered, Keller explained to them the next play. "We will pull the goalie early, do not drop the puck into the zone, play it, skate it in, we need just two goals, let's make sure we leave here with at least a tie."

At the drop of the puck Hatch dropped the gloves with another player in hopes to turn the game around and give his team mates a longer breathing session. The players skated back to the face-off circle.

Jackson calls the play: "Less than 90 seconds to go, Pythons gain possession and bring it up the neutral zone, Kilroy skates to the bench and Utica puts out an extra attacker, Hornets quickly snatch the puck back and here they come the other way, Pyle flattens him to the ice, but the puck is trickling towards the net, Lawless is racing after the puck, it's a slow race to the net, Lawless dives to swipe the puck out of its path, ohhh he did not reach it, the Hornets have scored the empty net goal to put this game away…and now it looks like we have some words being exchanged at center ice. Hatch is gonna go, it looks like he is fighting the player he just flattened, it's hard to tell since the press box here is up in the rafters." Hatch threw three times more punches in this fight, he pulled the jersey over the head of the player and started throwing hay makers. At the end of the fight, the fans booed him. He just put both fists into the air to the crowd, then motioned his invisible wrestling title belt around his waist. On the other end of the ice, Davidson started mouthing off to the entire New Haven bench, he threw a punch at one of the players and the whole bench stood up ready to go at him, Boone threw another punch at the other player and they both started exchanging punches. Both benches are standing up arguing with one another. The game finally ended and New Haven gets the victory with a 3-1 win over Utica.

The team boarded the bus to head back home. As the team left the city, Jared got up to the microphone in the front of the bus.

"I just want to say that, guys, keep your heads up. You have everything to be proud of. You did a great job, it was a long trip and we came out remaining well over .500, being only the first loss of the season. We are in first place and we are proud of every one who played hard. In thanks to playing great hockey, take tomorrow off, we will have a volunteer practice for anyone just wanted to keep fit. Great job tonight, guys."

Halfway home they stopped on the thruway to grab a midnight snack. They got off the bus, and went inside. The thruway stop had a Burger King and a Popeyes. Both were packed with people in line.

Roach turned to Pyle. "I have a plan, follow me, home-bread," Roach said as they walked out the front door. They went around to the back where the big drive-thru menu was.

"Vrooom, vroom!" Roach said, making sound effects that sounded very identical to a car engine.

"Like that is really gonna work," Scott said to him.

All of a sudden through the speaker. "Good evening, what can I get for you?"

Roach winked at Scott. "We need two grilled chicken specials and two Cokes," Roach said.

"Please drive up to the next window please." They got up to the window, the lady went to open the window and started laughing. "Where is your car?" she asked.

"We don't have a car, we just like to walk, it is good for the heart, eh!" Roach said. They took their meals and brought them back inside where their teammates were still in line.

Jared turned to them and asked, "How did you, where, what…never mind I don't wanna know."

They arrived back at the arena about 8 a.m. The players left for their cars to go back to their apartment. Kyle and Jared were picked up by their ladies. There was a mandatory press conference via the phone this morning with the league commissioner, Tom Krupe. Kyle and Jared sat at the table in the office. Sabrina and Renee got the coffee ready and brought some papers and pens.

She set up the conference speaker phone. "I hope we have some good news, every time we have these conference meetings they seem to bring down more bad news," Jared said.

The phone rang. "Utica Pythons call here," Sabrina said.

The voice muttered through the speaker. "Good morning from Brantford, Ontario. I am Tom Krupe and with me is the director of officiating Sam Brophy."

Kyle stood up. "Good morning, I am Kyle Tucker, with me is Jared Miller, and Sabrina our secretary of staff."

"Boys, we are gonna cut right to the chase," Krupe explained. "This is a respectable league, now we are all in favor of allowing fights, they are part of the game, and tempers flare, but this has absorbed national media attention in a negative way around the league," Krupe explained.

Jared stood up, so cutting to the chase, what are you saying?" he questioned.

The director of officiating spoke up. "What we are saying is that we will not tolerate a circus on league ice, the brawls are getting out of hand and the other teams are complaining and full of fear."

Kyle interrupted, "You can not sit here there and tell us how to play the game. We are not breaking any rules, nor are we breaking any league bylaws, we fight, we get penalized, that's it."

Krupe interrupted back, "Your organization is a disgrace to the league, and giving us a black eye, now either you ease up on your—"

Click. Kyle pulled the cord out of the machine. He was not about to allow the league to tell him how to play hockey, especially when no bylaws being broken or injuries occurred.

Kyle took his coffee cup and held it up to Jared. "I've always wanted to do that to that asswhip...Cheers!" They clinked their coffee cups together.

Chapter Ten: Hockey Season

"Welcome to the Snake Shack, I'm Marc Jackson," he said, introducing the TV show that he also hosted by the area news channel as well as doing the play by play for the games. "Sitting next to me is Pythons leading scorer, Scott Pyle, and, Scott, knowing this team is having such a great year thus far with a 14-3-1 record, do you think it is due to having the old school of hockey, especially with so much fighting?" Jackson asked.

Scott, scratching his forehead, said, "We have come together as a team and we will play together as team, the fights have always been a part of hockey, but I feel the tough guys do their part, I will do mine and that makes us bond as a team."

Jackson asked another. "What about yourself, you do a tremendous job shooting the puck between the pipes, but on the other hand, you are the only Pythons player that has not dropped the gloves this season, do you not approve of fights?" he asked.

Scott replied, "I have noticed the fans really like the fights, but they also like the goals obviously, I'm not saying I would never drop the gloves but if there was a situation that came about, I would if needed."

Jackson questioned, "The fans have been filling the arena to capacity, something that has never been done here before and it's all thanks to the two lotto boys that put you guys together, is this like the old Broad Street Bullies of the NHL?"

Scott kinda snickered and took a sip of bottled water. "Well, any hockey fan has a great deal of respect for the fearsome Flyers back in those days, how can you not, other teams were afraid to play them, and that's the message we are sending the FHL."

"Thanks for coming to join us today Scott!" Jackson said.

"My pleasure, eh!" he claimed.

Jackson went on, "Tonight the Pythons will be at home against the Cape Cod Trappers, they will be giving out free caps to everyone in attendance, seats are very limited."

Scott went off stage and through the exit door. "You fuckin' set me up, you assholes!" he yelled out furiously to the guys waiting for him by his truck.

It was Lawless, Roach and Hatch laughing hysterically. Roach mimicked him. "Eww…if the situation came about I would." They just laughed it off.

At the arena the people were lined up in the lobby to come inside for the game. Once they passed the turnstile every fan was given a free Pythons cap. They were dark blue with florescent green and black writing. The side said, "Old School Hockey," the back said, "Spectrum Logos," the sponsor giving the caps away. Jackson listed the lineup on the air. "Tonight is cap giveaway night at the Snake Pit Arena, wouldn't it be something if any of our players could score a hat trick, the hats would be tossed all over the ice…and it looks like we are in action already, the players lined up for the opening face-off, but just minutes later, Scott Pyle had scored on a breakaway and then scored again towards the end of the first period to give them a 2-0 lead." The fans were really anticipating that Pyle would score his third goal for the hat trick so they could toss them onto the ice.

Suddenly, nearing the end of the second period, Pyle had a one-on-one break, steered the puck into the Trappers Zone and shot on net, saved by the Cape Cod goaltender. Pyle quickly chased his shot in hopes of deflecting a rebound. The goaltender grabbed the puck and held on to it, took his waffle glove and slammed his glove into Pyle's face. Pyle threw his glove on hand into his mask.

Jackson called, "Just as we talked about this morning on TV, Scott Pyle just took a swing at the goaltender...ohhh, man...here we go, Pyle drops his gloves and is challenging the goaltender to fight...and he approves...and wait, a Trapper just jumped on Pyle from behind...and now a Pythons player jumps him...and it's a donnybrook on the ice!" Jackson was yelling.

The crowd cheered on Pyle fighting the goaltender behind the net. The fight lasted about a full minute or so before they were pulled from each by the linesman. The players were escorted into the penalty box. The crowd cheered him on in his first fight!

After everything was cleared up, the ref signaled for Pyle to go to the locker rooms being four minutes left in the period, there was no since for him to be sitting there. As Pyle left the box the entire Pythons bench started banging their sticks outside against the boards cheering him on.

The next period Pyle proved his wits, and now it was up to him to score the hat trick.

Jared radioed the coach. "Keep Pyle on the ice as much as you can, we need him to retaliate by scoring the hat trick."

Kyle and Jared knew every local media was here tonight watching the game. Pyle had the puck in front of the net, shot, wide. Lawless picked up the puck at the blue line, Davidson was right in front of the back up goaltender for Cap Cod. Just as Lawless passed it to the other to Pyle, Davidson took both his hands and cross checked the goaltender, the goaltender seen it coming and quickly squinted his eyes almost falling over backwards. Davidson totally faked him out not really intending to do so as he did not fully swing and hit him. Pyle took the slap shot from the top face-off circle, it deflected off a Trappers skate and into the fifth hole of the net!

"He sccoorres!" Jackson yelled into the microphone jumping up and down like a deranged fan. "Scott Pyle has done it, scoring a hat trick, his seventh of his career, and by God, you people at home have no idea what this ice looks like right now!" The Python fans were throwing hats all over the ice, it looked like a sea of blue. After the line went to the bench, Roach took Pyle's helmet off and told him to ware this. He gave him one of the caps, as he put it on, the crowd game him an ovation. He took a bow to the fans of thanks.

Kyle and Jared went back to the office the next morning. The secretary, Renee, gave Kyle a bunch of phone messages from the weekend. "Is this a fuckin' joke?" he asked her.

Jared grabbed the papers from him. "ESPN, Fox, ABC Sports and Sports Illustrated." He looked puzzled.

Renee looked up. "You guys are starting to be the talk of the country right now...take a look for yourselves," she said, turning to the TV. She started the tape, there the two ESPN commentators were showing the logo in the backdrop, and ESPN quoted, "Everyone's dream is to win the lotto, but to win the lotto, spend it on buying a minor league hockey team, and running it the way they want it? That's what two boys from a small city in NY State did. They changed the name from the Utica Snakes to the Utica Pythons and released all of their not so tough hockey players, and replaced them with the old school hockey players like the Broad St Bullies of the 70s and 80s.

"The NHL is trying to eliminate fighting altogether in hockey and says that is what fans like today. Well, maybe the NHL should go to Utica, NY, and start taking a look at the fans who really love the hard-nosed hockey games. The Utica franchise has had nine straight sellouts. Considering they used to be lucky to sell out one or two games all season long. The media is all over them like jam on bread. The fans love it, even the fans in other cities are coming out just to see this team and their goonish antics. Maybe old time hockey is making a comeback…eh," the announcer joked with the Canadian accent at the end of his cast.

Kyle and Jared just looked at each other and high fisted again. "Fuckin' eh!"

With the season rolling closer to spring, the Pythons have already clinched the playoff spot. The team was dominating the Federal League. The franchise was not only getting the attention of the league but the whole country of USA and Canada. The Hockey News weekly newspaper had a full two page write up on the franchise, the *Utica Post* listed them in the front page almost daily. The Pythons office had their web site being flooded with emails mostly to order souvenirs and merchandise that they had mostly on backorder.

Sabrina ran into the office jumping for joy. "Look at this, look, look!" she said, holding up the latest addition of *Vogue* magazine. It showed the home and away jerseys of the Pythons that she had designed herself.

The Pythons were now gearing up for the playoffs. They had easily clinched first place and have dominated the league from game one. They finished the season with a 56-11-5 record, first in the Federal League. On the ice they played solid hockey. The fights were adding up more and more, as other teams would fish out more tough guys, to help match up to the Pythons, which in turn they still out did their opponents. The difference was, the Pythons tough guys knew how to play hockey. They were not just "goons" as opponent's fans called them. Kyle and Jared picked the tough guys that could also handle the puck, check and were great at play making abilities.

Playoff fever was alive and rocking the arena. The Pythons have reached the semi-finals. One more win and they were on their way to the league championship. By now, the fans had many painted faces in the crowd and banners hung all over the walls of the arena rooting on the Pythons or bashing their opponents.

"Welcome back, Pythoners!" Jackson called on the radio. "The start of the third period is underway, the Pythons up 3-1 in front of another standing room only crowd. The Blast, in their orange, red and black uniforms, have control of the puck in their own end, and wham! Davidson just slammed Durbano of Saginaw into the boards and off his blades, Davidson picks up the puck, passes to Roach, over to Browstone, back to Roach, Roach brings it forward, fakes the pass, and shoots, he scccooorrrees!" Jackson exclaimed.

Roach pumped his arms into the air, and quickly skated over to the side boards where the glass was lower, and jumped onto the end of the boards holding on the glass, he started high fiving the fans in the front rows. It looked like the Packers Lambeau leap. The fans loved it, they went wild.

Jackson called it, "Darren Roach has done brought his crowd to a loud and wild frenzy, the place is going absolutely nuts. It is deafening here in da pit. I must say how impressed I am with Roach, when I was talking with him on his wild football antics and his purpose, he exclaimed to me how he does this for the fans…the fans are why they are here and the fans pay for excitement. There is no better way of acknowledging the fans and thanking them. The feel after it is unbelievable. Back to the game, face-off is at center ice with a Python 4-1 lead!"

Sitting behind the net was Commissioner Tom Krupe. Just shaking his head, and whispering to his partner. The fans counted down the last fifteen seconds of the game out loud.

"The Pythons are going where no Utica team has gone in over twenty years," Jackson cried out. "Five seconds, four seconds, three...Hey, Utica, whatya say. We're going to the Federal Cup Finals!"

Kyle and Jared sitting down in their usual section with their girls with them, were all hugging each other and jumping for joy. The arena just became a huge party atmosphere.

The Utica Pythons will now play a best of five series against the defending champion Baltimore Gulls. ESPN2 bought the rights of the Pythons to televise the games thinking that this is something that would go down in history. A team that has had one of the greatest records in minor league hockey history.

Tickets were sold out in advance, the media having a field day, and even a few of the buildings in the city had sheets hanging out of the windows saying, "Good Luck Pythons."

Game one being in Utica, the ESPN trailers were set up, the fans were lined up outside. One of the ESPN commentators interviewed Kyle. "What is it like owning a team and being so successful, after just ten months ago you were just a brewery worker?" he asked.

"It's the greatest feeling in the world, but we said for years that old school hockey was more exciting, more entertaining and more productive," Kyle said.

The commentator looked at him. "It more or less seems like you are trying to send a message to the NHL to show that fighting needs to stay in the game?"

Kyle claimed, "All I can say is take a look around you, eh, look at the fans, the media, the players, this is what hockey is all about, it has been for almost one hundred years. Why change it, eh?"

Chapter Eleven: Federal Funds

One week later, after a series of four games, the Pythons and Gulls had several upon several fights, hits, and four very low scoring games that have been very exciting. Each team had had great chances of scoring, and many special team situations.

"Welcome back to a special edition of the Snake Shack!" Jackson said, sitting in front of the camera of the TV news crew. "Tomorrow night we will witness the Federal Cup to be awarded to the winner. Something this city has not seen since 1981. The Pythons and Gulls are tied in a series at two games a piece, no holds barred, anything goes tomorrow night. ESPN2 will televise the game live again and I am sure even the NHL officials will be watching. The arena has just announced that they received permission from the City Coeds to add 400 more seats, behind the stage area end. Tickets will go on sale for those tomorrow morning at 9 a.m., limit of four per person."

The next day, people starting showing up in the arena parking lot around noon, seven hours before the puck is dropped. Everyone there was wearing Python souvenirs. People were having cook-outs, drinking beverages stored in coolers, playing hockey in the lots, some having pretend fights, and just getting pumped up.

By 6 p.m., it was almost like a rock concert again, people were lined up at the doors, banging on them, yelling to open up. Once inside, the fans filled up with merchandise of Federal Cup shits, caps, gloves, jerseys, you name it. The dasher boards had more writing on them but still no advertisements as they wanted that old style look still. One board said, "Good Luck Pythons," and "Thank you Python Fans," another said, "We Want The Cup." The penalty box for the visiting team was sponsored by Fonda's Flowers and was decorated all over with flowers. Also known to fans as the flower box.

Right after warm ups, the team went back into the locker rooms. Jared and Kyle were in there with them. The players just about ready to go on and Coach Keller walked in.

"This is what we have been fighting for nine months, guys. Look at you, with the black eyes, the stitches, the cuts, bruises, those are all carvings engraved in you showing you are a true warrior. We will win the war tonight, bash them, smash them and show them you can not come into our home and—"

"And you will do nothing of the sort if you want to play in this game," a voice said from behind. It was Krupe. He continued walking in. "Almost every hockey fan in this country and Canada will be watching this game tonight, and I will not have my league looking like a wrestling match."

Kyle stood up. "What the fuck are you saying, you can't change the fuckin' rules now."

Krupe looked at him at him grinning like the evil Grinch. "Oh you are very precise, Kyle, but I can tell the game officials to make more severe calls and watch the players more closely." He looked at the players who were all quiet and in shock over this. "Anyone dropping the gloves will not only receive a five minute major but a game misconduct as well. The refs will be calling anything they feel is inappropriate in the game, anyway, guys, I just wanted to say good luck to everyone. Ciao!" Krupe walked back out of the room, slamming the door.

"Can they do that shit to us?" Goalie Kilroy asked Kyle.

"Unfortunately in the bylaws of the league, they can not change the rules, but the can heavily enforce them," he said.

Roach stood up. "Fuck that fucking shit, man, are we gonna sit here and let them bitches tell us how to play? Hell fucking no! Let's go out there and play some bash 'em hockey!"

Jared shook his head. "We can't do that, man."

Lawless stood up. "We can not stoop to their level, are we gonna give up because of that asshole?"

Kyle spoke. "Ever hear the term don't play mad, play even? We will play hard, play old style hockey, but with no fights. Instead of throwing the fists, use our body as the fist. Slam your bodies in their face, we can still show them who owns the ice!"

Jackson continued with the play-by-play. "This is the moment we have been waiting for, my friends, the countdown has begun to the Federal Cup. The starting lineup has now been released, just looking over this, I...Baltimore...um..." Jackson turned to the ESPN broadcaster who was on a commercial break, and covered the microphone. "Is this correct?" he questioned. He nodded back. "Sorry, my friends, but we wanted to verify the info before announcing this, but it looks like Baltimore just jumped the old school hockey bandwagon, they have scratched three of their top five players, which sounds like good news...but the shocking part is they have added three players to their roster from the reserves. All three players played in the Steel League with over 200 penalty minutes each. All three players played the minimum regular season games to qualify for roster reserves. Well it looks like the players are taking the ice for Baltimore," he called.

The fans were booing loudly. The lights went down, and the announcer announced, "Python Fans...it is our building, it is our team, and it is our night tonight...let's welcome our Utica Pythons!" he growled proudly.

Jackson announced, "The Pythons are now taking the ice. They have refused to be introduced individually during the playoffs, in their beliefs that they want to be coming out as a team, not individuals, and the crowd is on their feet. I have never seen so many signs, painted faces and support in all my life. This is just extraordinary!"

ESPN went to a commercial break, and their first commercial, it was in the Pythons contract lease, was for the all new…Kyle and Jared's Beer Pops!

During the national anthem the place never went silent. The fans, knowing that they have never had a chance being on television, just kept on cheering and showing their loyalty chanting, "Let's go Pythons."

The ref went over to the players benches to give them a verbal warning sent down from the FHL Commissioner and skated away.

The teams lined up for the face-off. "And here we go, off the face-off," Jackson called.

"The Gulls take possession of the puck, bring it into the Pythons end, passed back to the blue line, Schultz has it for the Gulls, backhander, tipped wide." The Gulls seemed to have first control. Just minutes later, a Gulls player takes a slap shot from the blue line. His stick blade broke and both the puck and blade went towards the net. "What a horrible break," Jackson said. "Craig Kilroy had no clue for that split two seconds of which was the puck as both pieces came flying at him, the Gulls take the initiating 1-0 lead."

It was 2-0 Baltimore. Kyle immediately radioed to Keller.

He yelled, "What…it's only two goals, both were not his fault, they were flukes," he said.

Kyle grabbed the microphone part closer to his mouth. "I know it, coach, pull him…pull him just for a while. Put in the backup, give him a rest, and then switch goaltenders again."

It was a ploy that he felt could turn the game around. The coach just shook his head, he motioned for the goalie change. Kilroy came to the bench, threw his mask into the box. He was visibly pissed off, especially being in front of the home crowd.

The face-off lined up in the Python's end, talk was just getting started as a couple of the new tough guys Baltimore added, started talking shit. One of them looked at LeDruce. "You think you guys are tough now, well, you have met your fuckin' match tonight, hose face. Just try going after the puck, I dare you!" he said with both hands on stick ready for the face-off.

The puck dropped, LeDruce won the face-off, brought it behind the net, the Gull player checked him hard into the boards, as he fell, the Gull dropped his gloves and started pounding away at LeDruce who couldn't even get his gloves off. He barely even got to throw a punch. The linesman broke up the fight quickly and the two players went to the penalty box with eight minutes to go in the first period.

The ref blew the whistle and motioned for both players to exit the ice. The ref yelled, "Both get five for fighting and a game misconduct." The crowd recognized the motion of the ref before the announcement was made. Everyone was stunned and started booing.

"What the fuck call is that, you blind bastard?" LeDruce yelled. "I got fuckin' mauled out there and you're giving me a gamer?"

The ref just ignored him as they both went off the ice. The ref looked over behind the net and there was Commissioner Krupe just looking and smiling. Shortly after that, the play was deep in the Gulls zone, until another penalty was called, on the Pythons for interference. Then another, then another. The ref was not letting anything go.

At one time during the first period there were four players in the sin bin on each team. Both benches, barely any room to move. Late in the period, mostly four on threes or three on threes, the Pythons quickly scored on Lawless' slap shot from the point to cut the Gulls lead to one.

After the next play, a scrap ended up in front of the Python's goal. The back up covered up the puck when another Gull player fell on top. Each player grabbed on another. All five players were grabbing and shoving. The gloves dropped, and everyone paired off.

"We got another melee on the ice!" Jackson said with excitement. The fight lasted a couple minutes just as the first period was coming to an end. The ref signaled the Pythons bench to stay while the Gulls bench emptied to go to their respective locker rooms, then signaled for the Pythons once Baltimore was off the ice. This was to keep everyone in place and for nothing to get out of hand.

As the players took the ice at the start of the second period, the announcer read off the penalties. "Penalties for Baltimore to #13 Paul Jarvis, five minutes fighting and a game misconduct...#22 Stan Frasier, five minutes fighting and a game misconduct...#31 Frank Hanlon, two minutes leaving the crease, five minutes fighting and a game misconduct...#6 Gary Lemay, five minutes fighting and a game misconduct, and #27, Todd Henderson, five minutes fighting and a game misconduct."

The crowd was shocked but still cheering but not as loud as a normal cheer as most hockey fans there knew that the Pythons penalties would probably be just as bad.

The announcer continued. "Utica Pythons...#16 Sylvain Nasur, five minutes fighting and a game misconduct...#3 Derek Lane, five minutes fighting and a game misconduct...#19

Serge Huscroft, five minutes fighting and a game misconduct...#30 Bob Provencher, two minutes leaving the crease, five minutes fighting and a game misconduct...and #55 Darren Roach, five minutes fighting and a game misconduct."

The crowd was booing profusely. The players from both benches are standing in shock and yelling at the ref. The captains started yelling at the ref...the ref warned them if they continued they would be gone...but they didn't back down, they continued to protest, the ref signaled to the exit games...both players were given gross misconducts.

The game was since then started back up. Craig Kilroy back in net for Utica. Just minutes later a Gull player back checked one of the Pythons players into the boards. He went down hard, the ref blew the whistle. Five minute cross checking and a game misconduct for the Gulls winger.

The power play for the Pythons would help with three minutes left in the second period. The face-off being right in front of the Gulls bench.

"You wait, pal, it's your turn now!" one of the Gulls players told Lawless.

Lawless picked up the pass and shot the puck hard into the Gulls net! The sirens blew, the fog horn sounded and the spotlights flashing on the ice, the Pythons were back in it tying the game at two a piece.

Lawless, skating back over to his bench, passed the Gulls bench and laughed at them. One of the Baltimore players reached out and swung at him, he quickly retaliated and practically dove into the bench after that guy. It was about ten guys on one, the Pythons had no choice but to leave their bench to save their teammate. The Gulls bench was immediately filled with players half on and half off the ice fighting each other. Some of the players even were at center ice fighting. The crowd was going crazy again on their feet. "Fight for Your Right to Party" by the Beastie Boys was playing on the loud system.

After order was restored, the announced read the sheet filled list of penalties again. This time six more players, from each team, were handed game misconducts. The coaches were both yelling at the ref now. Some of the players wouldn't be escorted off the ice very easily, complaining about the calls. The ref called the period to an end. The remaining minutes would be tacked onto the third period again to try to restore order and get things under control. The fans were booing profusely and throwing cups and debris onto the ice.

Kyle and Jared were looking at each other in a huddle type. "How are they supposed to finish the game? There are some fourteen players now out of the game. We can't possibly have four players left to finish the remaining twenty minutes, they would never survive," Jared said.

They looked lost. The players went back to the locker room. Half of the players there were thrown out already and had half their equipment taken off.

Kyle and Jared came into the locker room. "I don't know what the fuck is happening but everyone get their equipment on, playing or not. Throw those jerseys back on, we are all still a team, no matter what, remember?" Kyle shouted.

Hatch looked at him and stood up. "We will be playing three on three for the next twenty minutes, those four players we have left will be dead."

Jared raised his fist. "Then we will die trying, won't we? Fuckin' eh, look at it this way, man, they have three players, we have the advantage. Just keep the puck passing and skate slowly. No big strides to wear yourselves down, it will be a long, long twenty minutes, but when it's all done, we will either be Federal Cup Champions, or we will be Division Champions. Either way, I want each and every one of you on that ice celebrating after the game, these fans deserve it as much as you guys do! Right now, almost every hockey fan is the country is watching this, it is the biggest moment in your career right now, so let's make it even bigger and more memorable."

The eight players remaining took the ice once the Zamboni completed the rounds. The fans were in shock still, seeing nothing like this before.

One of the fans looked at his friend sitting next to him sipping his beer. "How the hell is this game supposed to be finished with no substitutes left, no line changes and no breaks?"

The players lined up for the face-off. It was three on three, with a lot of open ice. One player in the penalty box for Utica, both teams has two forwards and a defenseman out on the ice.

The ref looked at the two before dropping the puck. "Just a warning from the commissioner, one more fight, and the game becomes suspended and no one will win this season."

Scott Pyle looked up at him. "We'll see about that!"

Jackson called the shots. "This should be very interesting as there are only eight players out on the ice and that includes the two goaltenders. This is absolute physical abuse. There is got to be some rule against this, or someone should put a stop to this. I just really don't see, folks, how these players will survive out there for twenty long grueling minutes, it is really inhumane."

Pyle lost the face-off. The Gulls got possession of the puck, passed it to the winger. It was a two on one break with the Pythons getting caught back, the Gulls brought the puck into the Utica zone, took a wrist shot from the face-off circle, and a split wide save by Kilroy. The crowd on its feet cheering them on.

The face-off back in the Pythons end of the ice with just 16:05 to go in regulation. Gulls win the face-off, passed it back to the defense, two Pythons shout after the puck, leaving a Gulls center wide open, the Baltimore defense slaps one on net from the blue line and deflected in off the center player. The Gulls now lead the game 3-1. The crowd getting more and more nervous, the players looking exhausted, taking line changes very, very slow. With 6:33 remaining in the game Baltimore had scored another goal on a three on one break giving them a commanding 4-1 lead.

Kyle and Jared were sitting in their section as usual. Kyle stood up and yelled to the guy two rows behind him, "Give me your binoculars…now, now!" The fan gave him the binoculars; he looked through them onto the ice. He quickly jumped over the fans' laps, practically falling on them to get to the aisle.

"Where are you going? What the hell are you doing?" Jared said as he tried to follow.

He ran to the other side of the stands radioing the coach. "Call the ref over!" he yelled.

The fans in that section noticed the coach getting radio contact. Coach Keller banged on the boards with a hockey stick to get the refs attention just before the face-off.

The ref skated over and looked at the coach. "Keller, you want a delay of game or a bench penalty?" The fans were quieter than ever wondering what was going on. The coach motioned over to #5 of the Gulls. The ref skated over to him, took his stick away from him and skated over to the time keeper's box. The ref grabbed a hockey ruler to measure. The fans started cheering knowing the plan Kyle and Jared had.

Jackson called, "What a genius plan, the Pythons are checking the Gulls player for an illegal stick. If the player is caught, he will serve a two minute minor for illegal stick. But don't get too excited, folks, if his stick is legal, the Pythons will receive a delay of game penalty. If this prevails, this could be a huge break for the remaining Pythons, and is a great way to rest for a minute or two…and now the ref is motioning the player into the box. It looks like he is going for an illegal curved stick, and Utica will receive a two minute power play!" Jackson got caught up in the moment forgetting that the Pythons were already down by three goals with less than four minutes remaining in the game. Jackson continued, "The Pythons would have to really start playing hard but to score three goals in four minutes is almost impossible. I'm not sure how they will do this Python fans but my guess is it would have to be a three on two or something. I've never seen this happen before. I don't know if it ever has ever happened but now it looks like the ref is skating over to the time keeper's box. I'm not sure what the discussion is about."

Kyle and Jared were right down there talking to the announcer over the glass and to the ref. Scott Pyle skated over to see what was going on. One of the other Gulls players skated over as well. In a huddled meeting the Gulls player skated away and swung his stick at the boards. The fans started yelling, not sure what was going on. The player skated over to the Gulls coach who in turn was now standing on the ice yelling at the ref.

The announcer got on the house public address: "Ladies and gentleman, I need your attention please." The fans didn't know if the Gulls player was getting ejected, or a call for security was going to be announced. "Penalty to Baltimore, #20, Mike Dunn, two minute minor use of illegal stick, two minutes unsportsmanlike conduct and a game misconduct. In accordance to the Federal Hockey League rules and regulations, the number of minimum players required on the ice at any given time is three skaters and one goaltender, the

Baltimore roster does not encompass the minimum required and is forced to forfeit the game under FHL rules."

The crowd erupted with a deafening roar. The announcer paused and then continued, "With an official 1-0 defeat, the Utica Pythons are the Federal Cup Champions!"

The announcement was practically screamed into the microphone. The ref handed Scott Pyle the giant shiny silver trophy that was skinnier than the NHL's Stanley Cup but a similar look. He hoisted it over his head and motioned his teammates standing in the locker room exit way to come out. They all charged out onto the ice, with all their equipment on except their gloves, stick and helmets. They had smiles from ear to ear, hugging and yelling, some had tears of joy over the excitement knowing that this will probably be the greatest moment of their career. Jared and Kyle went down on the ice and brought Sabrina and Renee with them. The ESPN cameras were also down on the ice. The ice was flooded with the players, coaches, owners, and media as the Python players skated the circle around the ice with the Federal Cup!

Darren Roach took the cup and skated over to the penalty box, went in and stood on the bench hoisting the cup over his head. "We did it, baby, we did it!" he yelled to the fans as they cheered him on.

The fireworks started shooting off above the ceiling lighting up the spectacle on ice. It was one of the most incredible scenes any hockey fan has ever witnessed in their lifetime. The music "Winners Take All" by Quiet Riot was playing over the sound system, a favorite of the boys.

ESPN was on the ice interviewing a couple players. "How does winning all this make you feel?" the commentator asked Pyle.

Scott, wiping the sweat from his forehead, had a big grin. "This is an incredible moment. I owe this all to my teammates.

We worked hard and made this all possible, and don't forget the two who brought us all together…Kyle and Jared," said Scott as he flagged them over.

The boys went in front of the ESPN camera almost in disbelief. "I still can't believe this is happening but all I can say is when you got a dream, go for it!" Kyle said.

The commentator asked, "What are you guys gonna do next?"

Kyle replied with a big smile, looking straight at the camera, "Something I have wanted to say for a while now but never knew the right time or place." Kyle looked at Sabrina standing next to him. "I have been waiting for this moment for as long as you have. I love you always, Sabrina, I would love to spend the rest of my life with you." Kyle pulled out one beautiful shiny gold engagement ring. Sabrina burst into tears, barely able to say the word "yes," but she managed. The two hugged heavily and as Jared and Renee jumped in on the group hug.

"Hey, guys, over here, let's go!" Hatch yelled to them from center ice. He was sitting on the ice with the rest of the team, for the winning team photo. They sat down next to the trophy and posed for what turned out to be the photo shot of the greatest moment in their lives.

Printed in the United States
89600LV00002B/13/A